THE BILLIONAIRE'S SECRET

A SWEET BILLIONAIRES ROMANCE

LORANA HOOPES

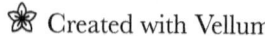

DEDICATION

To my family who lets me write the stories in my head.

To all the single parents out there - especially single fathers - You are doing a great job!

NOTE FROM THE AUTHOR

Thank you so much for picking up this book. I hope you enjoy the story and the characters as they are dear to my heart. If you do, please leave a review at your retailer. It really does make a difference because it lets people make an informed decision about books.

Sign up for Lorana Hoopes's newsletter and get her book, The Billionaire's Impromptu Bet, as a welcome gift. Get Started Now!

CHAPTER 1

 axwell Banks smiled at the buxom blond across from him. Her name had escaped his memory, but she would make a suitable companion for the night. The image of her long blond hair splayed like gold across his pillow filled his mind, sending his pulse into overdrive. Her yoga instructor body was just calling out for his attention if the tight shirt she was sporting was any indication.

Discreetly, he turned his wrist to check his watch. Fifteen minutes since they finished dinner. Surely that was a long enough segment of small talk. "You want to finish this somewhere more comfortable?" He reached across the table to stroke her hand as he said the words. A little flattery went a long way. He had mastered that art in the last few years.

Her tongue darted out and swiped across her lips, and her teeth bit the bottom one, causing the blood to flow to it and tint it a shade darker. "Um, sure, I guess that would be okay."

Her words were hesitant, and Maxwell knew he would have to turn up his charm. He didn't usually have to work hard to get women to come home with him. With his dark hair, blue eyes, broad shoulders, and chiseled chest his looks alone attracted many. The fact that he came from money attracted the rest. Those were the harder ones to get rid of, the ones after his money. They tended to show up uninvited and blow his phone up all hours of the day.

But this one wasn't looking for a sugar daddy. This one he picked up in yoga class. Yoga was not usually his thing; he preferred lifting and running, but his friend Justin had dared him to try the class, and as the instructor was hot, Maxwell had taken the chance.

He could tell when he entered the large room that she found him attractive as her eyes followed him as he crossed the room to grab a mat. His blue cut-off t-shirt had showed off his muscular arms and brought out his eyes, and his playing dumb had kept her by his side most of the class. Asking for her number had been easy after that. He had simply put on his puppy dog face and emphasized the need for private lessons if he was ever going to improve. She had fallen for it; hook, line, and sinker. Now it was time to seal the deal.

"Great." He whipped out his wallet and placed four twenties on the table. It was more than enough money as she only had salad and water—another perk to taking out weight conscious women. Then he stretched out his hand to her.

"Don't you need to wait for the change?" she asked, glancing around for the waiter.

"No, I believe in big tips." He flashed his best smile, hoping it would soothe some of the hesitation in her voice.

She shook her head in disbelief, but accepted his outstretched hand. He gave it a squeeze for good measure and then led her out of the restaurant and back to his black BMW Z4.

"What about my car? Shouldn't I just follow you?" She glanced around for her car in the full parking lot.

"Don't worry about it. I'll bring you back to your car later." Her smile relaxed as he opened the car door for her, and she slid into the grey leather seat.

After shutting her door, Max walked to the driver's side, folded himself into the driver's seat and turned on the engine. As the air had cooled considerably, he pressed the button for the heated seats before pulling out of the restaurant parking lot.

The girl—he really should remember her name—

pulled on her skirt to stretch it back down. It had crept up her leg revealing her smooth, toned thighs underneath.

"Can I turn on some music?"

Max mentally kicked himself. He'd been so distracted with her thighs that he hadn't realized they were driving in silence. Silence was never good. It let them think. "Of course, whatever you'd like."

She punched the buttons on the dial a few times before landing on some newer pop music. Inwardly, he cringed—he was more of a hard rock fan himself, but he knew the payout would be worth it.

Fifteen minutes later, he heard the sharp intake of her breath as he pulled into the driveway of his house. While not a mansion, the 4000-foot ranch home was impressive. The craftsman style boasted three slanted roofs, two chimneys, a grey-brick exterior, and a white wraparound front porch. A small working fountain sat in the middle of the circular drive.

"You live here?" The awe was plain in her voice.

He smiled inside. The deal was almost sealed now. "Yeah, it's a little big for one person, but I hope one day to fill it with a family."

When she turned back to him, he could almost see the stars in her eyes.

He pulled into the three-car garage and parked next to his Harley Davidson. The third bay contained no vehicle. At least not yet. The garage was neat as Max detested messes, and the few tools he owned meticulously lined the shelves along the wall.

Her heels clicked across the cement floor as he led her to the door into the house. It opened onto a large laundry room with a washer, dryer, and table to fold clothes on. The door from the laundry room led into the hallway. To the left was the kitchen, dining room, and family room. To the right were the bedrooms. Max turned left, leading her to where he had a bottle of wine waiting on the counter. It was yet another tactic he had learned would loosen women up and lower their inhibitions.

The large kitchen was half the size of the first floor of most houses. Stainless steel appliances filled the room, and a marble topped island in a crème color with brown and gold flecks sat predominantly in the middle of the room. A large silver light fixture hung above the island, and a deep sink took up a portion of the space under the light. The island hosted a bottle of red wine and two glasses, and across from the sink four plush barstools covered in black leather lined the island. The cabinets that circled the room were a deep brown, and a large walk-in pantry covered most of the back wall, but it was the wine Max focused on.

"Drink?" he asked as he uncorked the bottle and began pouring the glasses.

"Oh, I don't know if I should. I can't stay too long. I teach an early class tomorrow." The hesitation was creeping back into her voice, and her eyes darted around as if she might bolt. It was time to turn up the charm.

Max pushed his lower lip out in a slight pout. "You wouldn't make me drink alone, would you? Besides, what will one glass hurt?" The glass he extended to her was half full, and he focused his steely blue eyes on her. Many women had told him that his eyes were what drew them in, and Max knew how to use them to his advantage.

Her eyes flickered back and forth, but returned to his gaze, and he knew he had her. "Okay, maybe just one." Her arm rose and accepted the glass.

"To a wonderful night with a beautiful woman," he said, clinking her glass ever so slightly. A blush spread across her face, and she dropped her eyes to the murky red liquid as she took a sip. Max was about to suggest they retire to the living room, where his leather couch would be more inviting and conducive to his seduction, when the doorbell rang.

A glance at his watch revealed it was nearly ten p.m. No one he knew should be ringing his bell, and it was too late for solicitors. "Make yourself comfortable," he said to her, "I'll be right back."

As his shoes echoed on the hardwood flooring, he cursed the timing of whoever stood on the other side of the door. He had worked hard to get this woman here, and she had proven more skittish than many before her. If he lost her because of this interruption, there would be retribution.

Max was fully prepared to lash into the unfortunate soul on the other side of the door, but when he swung it open, his heart stopped, and his words failed him. The anger sizzled as if doused like a campfire, and he blinked not believing his eyes.

CHAPTER 2

"*S*arah?"

Though much paler and thinner than the last time he had seen her, Max was almost certain that the woman before him was the only woman he ever loved, the woman he lost three years ago without a word of explanation. Though he had been promiscuous before, it was her disappearance that had sent him into the philandering tailspin he'd been in for the last three years.

"Hi Max, can we come in?"

We? His eyes dropped lower to take in the small child clutching Sarah's hand in a death grip. She had dark brown hair and large blue eyes. Her daughter? But she didn't have a daughter when he was seeing her so that meant the girl must have come after she left. Not much longer though. Max was a terrible judge of age, but the child couldn't be younger than two.

Though every fiber in his body screamed for him to say no, shut the door, and return to his busty blond—who must be getting bored by now—he found himself opening the door wider. "Of course, come on in." He never could deny Sarah. In fact, though he never told her, he probably would have married her if she hadn't just up and left him.

Sarah and the little girl crossed over the threshold and stood, staring at him. "Can we go somewhere more comfortable so we can talk?" Sarah asked, tilting her head at him.

"Right, of course." He shut the front door and led them into the living room, completely forgetting the blond until she stood as they entered.

Her eyes shifted from him to Sarah and the child and back again. "What is this, Maxwell?"

"Uh, this is my friend Sarah, Sarah this is…"

The blonde's eyes widened as she realized he didn't know her name. "Seriously? You don't remember my name?"

Max cringed and shrugged. He should care; he didn't like getting caught, but Sarah had taken his attention. "Brigitte? Heather? Selena?"

The woman's face flamed red as her hands curled into fists and jammed into her slim hips. "Those aren't even close. It's Margo. I can't believe you." She pulled her purse strap tighter on her shoulder and shoved past Max, pausing to turn at the doorway. "Don't bother walking me out; I can find my own way home." The angry clomp of her heels echoed on the floor as she stomped to the front door.

Sarah turned her hazel eyes on Max. Her left eyebrow arched on her face. "I see some things haven't changed."

"What can I say?" he said, shrugging again. "Women find me irresistible, and there are too many to remember all their names."

Sarah shook her head back and forth. "I'm not sure this was a good idea."

"No, wait." Max's demeanor straightened as he reached out to stay Sarah. "Tell me why you're here."

"Sweetie, why don't you go in the living room and play while I talk to Max?" The little girl responded with wide eyes and a silent head shake. "Go on, you have your tablet. I'll be right in here." Reluctantly, the little girl let go of Sarah's hand and trudged into the living room. A tattered backpack hung from her thin shoulders.

As Sarah sat in one of the barstools, Max noticed the dark circles under her eyes and the hollowness of her cheeks. What had happened to her? He eased himself onto the stool next to her and waited for her to speak.

Sarah's frail shoulders rose with her inhaled breath, and she forced her eyes to Max's. "I guess there's no easy way to say this, but I'm dying. I have anaplastic carcinoma. There's a cancer hospital in New York that specializes in treatment for my condition, but I'll be too weak to watch Peyton. You know I have no other family, and"—she looked into the living room where the girl was curled on one of the couches playing a tablet before turning her attention back to Max — "Peyton is your daughter, so I'm hoping you'll take her in."

Her words hit him like a truck, shaking any response from his mind. She was dying? He had a daughter? When he could finally wrap his mind around it, the words came out small and quiet. "Why didn't you tell me about Peyton before?"

She tilted her head at him as if she couldn't understand why he would even ask that. "Maxwell, you always told me you weren't one for settling down, and the day I was going to tell you, you told me about your friend Justin being trapped into a relationship with a pregnancy and that he was going to push the woman to have an abortion."

Maxwell's eyes dropped. He remembered the conversation. Justin was as much of a philanderer as he was, maybe even more so. Justin had taught him a few trade secrets, and it was true that the few times he had ended up getting a woman pregnant, he forked over the five hundred dollars for the abortion rather than being sucked into a relationship or fatherhood. But Maxwell wouldn't have pressured Sarah into that, would he have?

"I couldn't take the chance you would do the same, as I wasn't strong enough to fight back because I loved you so much. I probably would have agreed just to keep you, and then I would have hated us both, so I left."

"Does she know?" Max asked, shrugging towards the little girl in the other room. He was still having trouble grasping the gravity of Sarah's words.

When Sarah smirked, he saw a glimpse of her old playful nature. "That I'm dying or that you're her father?" Then her face grew serious. "Yes, she knows both. She isn't excited to be left behind, but she understands I have little choice. It's either you or foster care, and she is more inclined to try you than a total stranger not related to her."

"But, Sarah, I'm no role model for a little girl."

"So I see, but I took that into consideration." She reached into her purse and pulled out a card. "This is my best friend's number. She has known Peyton since she was a baby, and she can help you out if you need anything."

"Then why doesn't she just take her?" Maxwell didn't mean for the words to come out as catty as they did, but the thought of being left alone with the little girl —even if she was his—terrified him.

Sarah's brow furrowed. "Because she is still going to school and can't afford a full-time nanny. You can. And because you're her father. I've never asked you for anything, but I'm asking you now." She reached across and clasped Maxwell's hand. "Be a dad. For once in your life, stop thinking about yourself or your next easy woman and think of someone else for a change. Peyton needs you. I need you."

The words cut him to the quick. Her directness and unwillingness to put up with his crap were two things he loved about Sarah. "You should have told me about her sooner," he said and found that he meant it.

"You're right. I should have. We both made some mistakes, but none of those mistakes are Peyton's fault. She's a good girl, Max. She's a lot like you when you aren't trying to be suave and debonair."

"I thought you liked my suavity and debonairness," he said with a crooked, sexy smile.

"No, I hated those two traits. I liked you for the man you are when you take off the masks, and one day, if you can keep those masks off, you'll find another woman who will feel just as I did."

Her words sobered him and wiped the smile off his face. "Do you have a chance?"

A small, sad smile played across her lips. "There is always a chance, but it doesn't look good. The cancer spreads quickly, and we may not have caught it in time.

I'm going to give the doctor's a chance, but at this point, I think it would take a miracle from God."

God? She hadn't been religious in the past, and he wondered if her cancer had made her seek solace in fairy tales.

"Here," she reached into her bag, pulled out a notebook, and handed it over to him. "I've written down Peyton's schedule, her bedtime routine, her fears, and what calms her down. I hope it's all you'll need, but again Alyssa can help. She's expecting your call whenever you might need to make it."

As she pushed herself up from the barstool, his heart tightened. "Wait, you're going now?"

"I have to; I have a plane to catch. I have a few more bags for her in the car. I'll set them on the front step before I leave." Sarah looked past Max and called, "Peyton, come here please."

The little girl appeared by her mother's side, so quiet it was almost stealthy. Sarah knelt until she was face to face with the girl. "Peyton, Max is going to take care of you, but he might need some help. Be patient with him and help him out."

Peyton's big blue eyes filled with tears, and she wrapped her arms around Sarah's neck. "I don't want you to go, Mommy."

"I know, Baby, and I don't want to go, but it's Mommy's last chance to get better."

As the two hugged, Max felt a stirring in his soul that he'd never felt before, but too soon, Sarah was standing again, and the little girl was crying big hitching sobs as tears streamed down her cheeks.

"I love you, Peyton," Sarah said, and then she was gone, and Max was left staring at the small girl. What was he going to do now?

CHAPTER 3

*A*s the sunlight streamed in the bedroom window, Max opened his eyes, hoping the previous night had been a bad dream, but as he rolled to his left side, he saw the little girl curled up with her pink bear clutched tightly in her arms. Her long lashes fanned out on her cheeks, and she looked peaceful as her little chest rose and fell, but he knew that wouldn't last long.

Last night after Sarah left, the little girl had been almost inconsolable. She had cried for an hour straight while Max awkwardly hugged her and tried to offer her books or movies—he had no toys, and she hadn't brought many with her. He had finally decided to lay her down, but she hadn't wanted to stay in his guest room either, so he had nestled her in his own bed and laid with her until she had fallen asleep.

As quietly as possible, Max edged out of bed and headed into the kitchen for coffee. It had been a long night, and he had the feeling today would be a long day too. As he passed the front door, he remembered Sarah saying something about putting more bags on the front porch. He had forgotten all about them last night, but thankfully they were still there when he opened the door. After bringing them inside and locking the door once again, he continued his trek to the kitchen. His cell phone rang just as the coffee started percolating.

"Hey, man, we still on for tonight?" Justin's voice carried through the phone.

Max sighed. He had forgotten all about their plans for the evening. "I don't know. Something happened last night, and I have to take care of some stuff."

"Stuff? What are you talking about? This party is going to be epic."

Max grabbed a mug from the cabinet and filled it with coffee. "Sarah showed up last night."

"Sarah? The girl from four years ago? What did she want?"

"She wanted to introduce me to my daughter."

Justin let out a long, low whistle. "Daughter? Are you sure? Did you ask for a paternity test? I know you liked her, but she could just be trying to trap you, man, get some money, you know?"

Max hadn't considered asking for a paternity test,

partly because it was Sarah, and he couldn't believe she would come back for money, but also because the girl looked like him. She had his nose and his blue eyes. He had no doubt she was his.

"It's not like that. She's dying, and she needs to get treatment, so she left Peyton with me until she either gets better or..." He trailed off. If Sarah didn't get better, that would mean Peyton would be his responsibility forever. What had he agreed to?

"That's heavy, man, what are you going to do?"

Max took a sip of the hot coffee and shook his head though he knew Justin couldn't see the motion. "She left me the number of her friend. I'm going to call her today and see if she can take care of this."

"Maybe her friend will be hot, and it will be worth it."

Max rolled his eyes. Justin should know better than to mix business with pleasure. "Yeah, maybe. I'll let you know." Max hung up the phone before Justin could add more. He took another sip of his coffee and almost dropped the mug when he saw Peyton. Again, he had not heard a sound.

"Hi, Peyton, you hungry?" he asked, pasting on what he hoped was a smile. "I think I have cereal or we could go get breakfast." What did three-year-olds even eat?

"I want my mommy."

"I know you do," he said, kneeling to her level as

Sarah had last night, "but Mommy had to go away for a while."

"I want her back." She stepped to him and threw her arms around his neck. Last night, she had barely let him touch her, so the force of her hug threw him off guard and off balance.

She smelled sweet and innocent. It was such a different smell from what he was used to that he wasn't sure he could explain it if he had to. Without thinking, his arms wrapped around her, and his hands began to pat the soft brown curls of her hair. It was an awkward and unfamiliar gesture. He didn't even like to console the women he dated, and he could feel his shoulder getting wet from her tears.

"Peyton, I know you miss her, and I am a lousy replacement, but I'm going to need your help, so can you try to be a big girl and stop crying?" His words did not have the desired effect as a loud screeching noise began to accompany the sobs.

Crap. What do I do now? He remembered the card with Sarah's friend's name on it and untangled himself from the child to search for it. The counter. Sarah had laid it on the counter. Thankfully, he was a neat freak and his counter was clutter free. The white card called like an SOS beacon from the same spot Sarah placed it last night.

Scooping it up, he perused the information. Alyssa

434-555-1347. The screeching had gotten louder and shriller from Peyton, and he nearly dropped his phone in his haste to extricate it from his pocket the first time.

Please be home. Please be home. The mantra ran through his head as he input the digits. Though it felt wrong to leave Peyton alone, he headed down the hall and away from the kitchen, so when Alyssa hopefully picked up, he would be able to hear her.

"Hello?" The voice was soft and feminine—music to his ears—but not for the usual reasons.

"Is this Alyssa?" His own voice sounded strange in his ears—desperate and high pitched.

"It is, to whom am I speaking?"

The properness in her return gave him pause, and he blinked trying to re-form the words he had seconds ago. "My name is Maxwell. Sarah gave me your number and said you could help with Peyton. She's crying—well, screaming is more like it—and I can't make her stop. Is there a trick? Can you help?"

A small chuckle met his ears. "There is no magic pill you can give her. She's lost her mom. You have to learn how to console her. Hug her and let her know you are there for you."

"I tried that," he said, the desperation now clawing at his throat. "It only made her cry louder."

"You have to give it time," she said, "but give me

your address, and I'll swing by. It sounds like you are out of your element here, and I'd like to make sure Peyton is taken care of."

CHAPTER 4

*A*lyssa hung up the phone and grabbed her keys. Sarah had told her to expect a call from Maxwell, and while she hadn't expected it so soon, she was curious to see what this man was like. The stories she had heard from Sarah had her intrigued to say the least.

Half an hour later, she pulled up in the grand driveway, and her eyes widened. Sarah had said he was wealthy, but the appearance of this house made *wealthy* an understatement. Alyssa was sure she was going to feel underdressed in her jeans and "I love Paris" t-shirt.

Not bothering to lock her car door—she had nothing worth stealing compared to this house—she dropped her keys in her purse and approached the massive front door, which was actually two large wooden doors with an ornate gold trim. She pressed the bell, curious as to what the inside would hold.

Alyssa was surprised when, a moment later, the doors opened and Max himself stood on the other side. At least she assumed it was Max. He wore no uniform, just a pair of cargo shorts and a t-shirt. His dark hair was tousled as if he had just woken up, but it was his piercing blue eyes that convinced her. Sarah had spoken of these blue eyes often, but even her description held no candle to the effect they had in person.

"Maxwell?" Alyssa asked, tilting her head and holding out her hand.

"You must be Alyssa," he said, shaking her hand. It was strong, but not rough. He must not work with them much. Sarah had never mentioned his job, but looking at Maxwell, Alyssa could see why. His physical appearance dominated her brain.

"Yes, sorry, I was just expecting someone else to answer the door. The house is so large; you must have some help." Her eyes scanned the foyer behind him. It was clean and minimalist, decorated in browns and creams.

"I don't keep full-time help," he said, dropping her hand. "I like my privacy."

Though Alyssa nodded, she couldn't imagine one wouldn't still have privacy in a place this big even with full-time help. "Where is Peyton? May I see her?"

Maxwell stepped back, scooting boxes aside with his foot, and motioned her inside. "She's in the living room. It took forever to get her calmed down enough to eat, but a frozen waffle and some cartoons seemed to have helped."

Maxwell led the way through the ornate foyer and down a hall into the living room. Alyssa tried to keep up, but her attention was drawn to the left and the right as they meandered through the house. She wasn't sure if his artwork was genuine, but the sheer amount of famous paintings hanging on his walls was enough to awe her.

A large television screen hung on the living room wall, displayed an episode of Sophia the First. Peyton was curled into one corner, her bear snuggled tightly to her chest. She looked smaller than her three years on the large leather couch.

"Hey, Peyton, how are you?" Alyssa asked, as she sat down beside her.

Peyton turned big blue eyes up at her. They weren't quite the same blue as Maxwell's, but it was clear the gene came from him. "Hi, Aunt Lyssa. I miss my mom."

"I know, sweetie, but your mom is going to get treatment to see if she can get better. Has Maxwell been taking care of you?" Alyssa could feel Maxwell staring at her back, but she kept her eyes focused on Peyton, who shrugged.

"I guess. He didn't want to read to me last night, or pray, or sing, though."

"I don't sing," Max chimed in.

Alyssa shot him a silencing look. "Well, Peyton, Max isn't used to having a little girl in the house, and he doesn't know the routines, but I bet you could help him."

"Okay, I'll try."

As her attention turned back to the screen, Alyssa rose from the couch and motioned Max to follow her to the kitchen where they could speak privately.

"You have to try to follow her routine," she said as she placed her hands on her hips. "She just lost all stability in the world. Those routines are the only thing grounding her."

Max crossed his arms, and Alyssa's eyes were drawn to the well-toned appendages. "Maybe you should take her. I don't know how to be what she needs."

"I would if I could, but I have to finish school. Besides, you're her father. If Sarah doesn't get better, you'll be her custodian legally. Show me her room."

"Her room?" Max blinked at her as if her words were not computing in his brain.

"Yes, her room. Where she will be sleeping."

"She just got here last night, and she didn't want to stay by herself, so she ended up in my room."

"She can't stay in your room. She needs a proper

room. Show me your guest rooms then, and we'll work on fixing one up for her, so she feels comfortable."

"What do you mean fixing one up?" There was a hint of panic in his voice, which Alyssa couldn't decide if she found annoying or charming.

"I mean paint, a kid's bed, toys." As his eyes widened in alarm, she pointed her finger at him. "Unless you want to be sharing your bed with a three-year-old for the foreseeable future."

Max took a step back and shook his head. "Fine, you can decorate a room. Follow me."

He led the way back down the hallway toward the foyer.

"What are these boxes? Are they Peyton's?" she asked as he passed them again as if they weren't there.

He shrugged. "Yeah, Sarah left them last night."

"Why haven't you opened them?"

"To be honest, I forgot about them until this morning."

"Well, you should un-forget, and when we get her room figured out, we should unpack them for her. That would help. She needs familiar things to help her get through this."

Max rolled his eyes but nodded. "Fine, we'll unpack them later. Do you want to see the rooms or not?"

Alyssa swallowed her agitation and motioned for him to continue showing the way. They crossed through the foyer and down another hallway. Three doors lined the hallway on the left and right plus a door sat at the end.

Grasping the handle, Max swung the first door on the right open. A spacious bedroom lay on the other side with a queen bed and a large dresser. Nothing else was in the room, not even a book or a lamp.

"Don't use this one much, huh?" Alyssa asked, surprised by the sterility of the room.

"Don't use any of them much. It's just me, remember?" He opened the next room which was very similar to the first. The third door was the first-floor bathroom.

"Well, I can see why she didn't want to stay in either of those rooms. They are impersonal at best and probably scary to a small child. We need to go get some paint, a smaller bed, and toys. Are you free now? I have some time."

"Yeah, I guess," he said shrugging. He closed the doors, and they returned to the living room to grab Peyton.

As they entered the garage, Alyssa looked around. Her brow furrowed as she turned to Max. "Where is your car?"

"What do you mean? It's right there," he said pointing to the BMW.

"You can't take Peyton in that. There's no backseat. Where would you even put a car seat in there?"

He blinked at her. "A what?"

Alyssa rolled her eyes. Had this guy been living under a rock? "A car seat. Kids have to use them until they are old enough or tall enough to sit in a booster seat, which also wouldn't fit in your car. Children can't sit up front because of the airbags. Your car is a deathtrap."

Max's face turned to stone and his arms crossed. "My car is a work of art. It goes zero to sixty in less than six seconds."

A short burst of irritated breath flew out of Alyssa's mouth. "A three-year-old doesn't care how fast your car goes. She cares about being safe in your car. Never mind," she said, shaking her head, "we'll take mine."

"You have a car seat in yours?" The comment was snide and meant to get under her skin, but Alyssa chose to ignore it and closed her eyes for a moment before answering.

"No, I don't have a car seat in my car, but at least it has a back seat. Didn't Sarah leave Peyton's car seat?"

"Not unless it's in one of those boxes by the front door," he said.

"No, it would be bigger than those boxes. She must have forgotten. Well, we can strap Peyton in my backseat, and I will drive very carefully to a store where we can get a car seat for her." Alyssa looked down at Peyton who had been quiet during the exchange. Her eyes turned expectantly to Max as if she had been following them like an unseen tennis match.

"Fine, we'll take your car, but I'm not getting rid of my BMW." He hit the garage door button, and the bay began to lift, allowing them access to her car in the driveway.

"With your money, you could just buy another car," Alyssa said under her breath as she grabbed Peyton's hand and followed him. She couldn't believe the nerve of this man nor could she understand how Sarah was ever attracted to him. Sure, he was good looking, with his dark hair and tempting blue eyes, and he obviously took care of his body as his shorts hugged his frame just right and his arms displayed the lines of finely toned muscles, but he was just as self-absorbed as he was handsome, and that was a trait she could not stand.

Max stopped short at the sight of her blue Ford Escort. "You want me to ride in that?" he asked as his head dropped forward in disbelief.

Alyssa pulled her shoulders back. Her car might not be a convertible sports car like his, but it was reliable and hers. Through dedication, she had managed to pay it off while going to school. "There's nothing wrong with *that*," she said pointedly. "My car is safe and reliable."

"And boring," he said in a sing-song lilt.

Letting the comment go, Alyssa opened the back

door for Peyton and strapped her in. "I promise I'll drive safely, Peyton."

Still grumbling under his breath, Max climbed into the passenger seat, and after strapping herself in the driver's seat, Alyssa started the car and pointed it in the direction of the nearest Wal-Mart.

"I cannot shop here," Maxwell said as she pulled into the discount store parking lot.

Exasperated, she rolled her eyes at him. "You can, and you will. They have everything we need here, and I don't know where the nearest hoity-toity store is that would have what we need."

The look on his face led her to believe that no one had ever talked to him that way, and it gave her a small amount of masochistic pleasure to see him put in his place.

After rescuing Peyton from the back of the car, she placed her in the front section of the shopping cart and fastened the strap.

"Is that really necessary?" he said over her shoulder, pointing to the strap.

"Every time." She said the words, slow and pointedly, hoping they would sink in his thick skull. "I've heard stories of kids standing up and falling out of the carts while their parents' backs were turned. If you keep them buckled that never happens."

Max shrugged. "If you watch them close enough, it also never happens."

"Yeah, and I'm sure that would be your specialty if she were twenty-three instead of three."

His eyes narrowed into a glare at her, but he said nothing as they made their way into the store.

Alyssa walked the store as if she owned it, steering the cart directly to the baby aisle where she began perusing the options of car seats. Max stared at the variety as if the sheer amount of options had never occurred to him. "That one," she said pointing to a red and grey Graco convertible seat.

"Why that one?"

"Because she can use it up to one hundred pounds, which means it should last you a few years."

"Years? How long do kids have to ride in car seats?" He hefted the box and slid it onto the bottom of the cart.

"Until they're old enough or weigh enough not to. You should look up the rules now that you'll have her full time." Her lips pursed as she tapped a finger to the side of her mouth. "Next, baby monitor."

Max's forehead furrowed. "Baby monitor? What for? She's three."

"And if you lived in a normal house where you could hear her, I'd say maybe you're right, but you live in the flipping Taj Mahal, which means you wouldn't hear her cry out if you were on the other end of the house, so you need a monitor."

"Fine. Lead the way." The words were tight and forced through clenched teeth. His jugular bulged out on the right side and put another little smile on Alyssa's face.

After the monitor, they picked out a bed. Even though it was broken down and in a box, there was no room in her car to carry the bed, so they arranged to have it delivered. Then she wheeled him through the clothes, picking up a few more things for Peyton. She knew Sarah hadn't packed all her clothes; she also knew Sarah hadn't had much money for clothes recently.

The toy aisle was next, and while she didn't want to overwhelm Peyton, the girl deserved a few toys, puzzles, and of course bubbles. Every time Alyssa visited, Peyton wanted to drag her outside and blow bubbles. The last stop was the hardware section for some paint and brushes.

By the time they wheeled up to the checkout line, the cart was overflowing. Alyssa almost felt bad for the amount of money Max was about to spend, but then she remembered his house and how he treated Sarah, and she decided he could afford it.

CHAPTER 5

*A*s they pulled up to his house, Max glanced over at Alyssa. As much as she annoyed him, he had to admit she had been helpful as well. Not only had she helped him figure out which car seat to buy, but she had also picked out the bed, some clothes, and a cart full of toys. He was not much of a shopper himself, unless it was for cars, but she seemed to have been right in her element. Had she helped Sarah do all of this when Sarah first found out she was pregnant?

If he was honest, it also intrigued him that she stood up to him. He couldn't remember the last time a woman had since Sarah, and he found it interesting. Not that he would ever consider dating her; she was far too uptight, though she was gorgeous with her long dark hair and her bright green eyes, but she would be too much work. Still, he had learned a lot watching her with Peyton today.

"Peyton and I will take the clothes and toys in and unpack her room," Alyssa said, forcing his attention back to the present. "Why don't you try to fit her car seat in your BMW?" A sly smile played across her face as she said it, like she knew it wouldn't fit, but Max was determined to prove her wrong.

"Fine," he said. After fumbling with the strap but finally unhooking Peyton from the contraption, he placed her down on the ground and reached in for the handles he knew Alyssa clipped to something. Though he could feel the bulky plastic, he couldn't seem to get it unfastened.

"Here," Alyssa said, leaning in from the other side of the car. She placed her hand on his and guided it to the release button. Though he heard the click, his focus was on her hand, which still laid across his own. It was smooth and pale, like fine porcelain, and was causing a warmth to spread across his hand.

His eyes found hers, and there was a spark, a connection that wasn't there before. She pulled her hand back as if the warmth he felt were a fire to her, and the moment was broken. Shaking his head, he unhooked the other side of the car seat and finagled it out of the car.

Alyssa stood, several bags hanging from her arms. She glanced at Max before heading into the open garage, Peyton trailing behind her. Max watched her go, wondering what that connection had been. He couldn't be developing feelings for her. It would be too complicated.

When Alyssa and Peyton were safely inside the house, he carried the car seat to his car. As he opened the passenger door, he could see Alyssa was right. Not only did the car seat not fit, but there were no hook things like there were in her car for the seat to attach to. He hated the fact that she was right and even more the fact that he would have to buy a new car. He hadn't been planning to purchase a new vehicle, least of all, a family car. He'd have to see if he could get Alyssa to watch Peyton as he couldn't very well take her with him in his car. The good news was that he could hit the party while he was out, and Alyssa could stay and watch Peyton.

After placing the car seat against the wall of the garage, he headed inside to find Alyssa. He realized she was right about the monitor too as he stepped inside the quiet house and turned toward the bedrooms. If he hadn't known they were there, he would never have guessed it from the lack of noise.

He found them in the first guest bedroom. Alyssa had unpacked Peyton's small backpack and the boxes that had been sitting by the front door and was folding the clothes, placing them in the dresser while Peyton played with her bear and a new doll on the floor.

"Can you watch Peyton for a little longer?"

"Why? What's the problem?" Though she posed them as questions, he could hear the teasing inflection in her voice.

Biting his lip to keep from smiling, he crossed his arms and leaned back. "You know very well what the problem is. The car seat won't fit, and I need to go get a different car. Can you watch her while I do that? I can pay you."

"Oh, I know you can, but there's no need for that. Knowing I was right is payment enough." She smiled sweetly at him. "Though if you wanted to bring back some pizza for dinner, I wouldn't argue with that."

"Yeah, pizza," Peyton said, offering him a genuine smile.

"I don't know how long it will take, but I'll leave money for pizza on the bar."

After placing forty dollars on the counter, he climbed into his BMW and checked his watch. If he was quick at the dealership, he should still be able to hit the party before all the good women were hooked up.

The dealership was just about to close as he pulled in. Salesmen were locking the cars and driving them back to the display spaces.

"Hey," he called to one of the overweight salesmen as he parked his BMW. "Who's in charge? I need a car, and I have money to spend."

The man's tired demeanor disappeared at the word "money," and his eyes lit up. He even tried to smooth the wrinkles out of his Hawaiian shirt to make his appearance more presentable. "Roger is in charge, but I'll be happy to help you out."

"Good. I need a sedan. I don't even really care which one as long as it's safe, and it has those hooks to fasten a car seat in."

The large man smiled widely. "Oh, a new dad, huh?"

"Yeah, something like that." Maxwell wished the man would just take him to the cars. He was in no mood for small talk and he wanted to get this done so he could get to the party.

"Okay, well our best family car is the Chevy Malibu. It comes with the Rear Seat Reminder system, so you never leave a child in the back seat accidentally. Plus, it has Apple Play for when they get older."

"That sounds perfect," Max said, though he had no idea what either of those actually were.

"Don't you want to see it first? Drive it?" the salesman asked, as he blinked at Max.

"You said it's your best family car, right?"

"Yes, but everyone has their own opinions," the man stated.

"I trust yours. Get me a blue or a black one and let's wrap this deal up."

The salesman's eyes narrowed as if he was trying to decide if Max was pulling his leg. "Alright," he said, obviously deciding Max was the real deal, "let's go meet Roger to start the paperwork, and I'll get you the best one on the lot."

Max followed the salesman into the office. Most of the other men were packing up, but one man sat at a large desk near the back. Though plump in the middle, Max could tell from his arms that he still worked out.

"Roger, this is... I'm sorry I didn't catch your name."

"Max, Maxwell Banks."

"Maxwell Banks of Banks Inc.?" the salesman asked, his eyes wide.

Max bristled. Ever since his parents tried to force their newly acquired religion on him a few years ago, he hadn't been on speaking terms with them. "Yes, that's me, well, my father, I guess, but it's my family."

"We're so glad you stopped in Mr. Banks," Roger said, rising from his desk. "I'm sure Paul here helped you out, but what can I do for you tonight?"

"Paul suggested a Chevy Malibu, so he brought me in to start the paperwork while he gets me the best one on the lot."

"Of course," Roger said, sitting back down and motioning to a chair across from him. "Please have a seat, and we'll get you taken care of."

"Thanks, Paul," Max said to the salesman as he

hurried out of the office and back to the lot. "I'll need this delivered tomorrow to my house. That won't be a problem, right?"

"Not for you, Mr. Banks," Roger said. Max could see the dollar signs flashing in the man's mind.

Less than an hour later, Max had signed the paperwork and left his address and an extra five hundred dollars to have it delivered the next day. Now to hit the party.

The party was already well underway when Max stepped inside. He scanned the crowd, finding Justin snuggled up with a blond in the far-right corner. As he made his way that direction, he garnered the attention of a pretty red-head. A quick glance revealed a stunning body, and he hooked an arm around her waist, propelling her with him towards Justin.

"Hey man, I didn't think you were going to make it." Justin untangled himself enough to shake Max's hand.

"Yeah, me either, but an opportunity presented itself. Never look a gift horse in the mouth, am I right?"

"Well, pull up a chair and we'll get more drinks." Justin pointed to the open chair across the table.

Max looked around for a second chair, but the place was packed. Deciding they could share the chair, he sat down and pulled the red-head onto his lap. She took no time in leaning forward and claiming his lips.

"My name is Liza," she whispered seductively in his ear, after tracing her lips across his cheek.

"Pretty." He made no attempt to remember her name. He wouldn't be seeing her after tonight, but for now he enjoyed the feel of her against him.

"So, how's the friend?" Justin asked, when Liza let Max come up for air.

"A handful, but serving a purpose." Max winked at Justin, hoping he would get the meaning.

Justin smiled and nodded.

"Let's take this back to your place," Liza whispered in Max's ear.

"I can't," he said, running his hand through her hair. "My place is being renovated. How about your place?"

She shook her head. "Roommates."

"Hotel?" He didn't normally shell out extra money, but extenuating circumstances called for extraordinary measures.

Liza stood and held out her hand. It was all the invitation Max needed.

"See you next week." Max flicked a mock salute at Justin and then led Liza to his car.

"*W*here have you been?" The anger in Alyssa's voice was unmistakable, though it was punctuated by her crossed arms and narrowed eyes.

"Getting a new car, remember?" Max hung his keys on the hook and turned to face her.

"Uh huh, do all new cars come with lipstick?" Her eyes flashed with each word.

Lipstick? He knew he wiped his mouth, but his hand touched his lips just to be sure.

"Not there," she said, advancing on him. "There." She ran her finger across his neck and held it up. A slight red smudge was smeared across it.

Dang it. He forgot to check his neck.

"I can't believe you would go out on a date with your daughter here all alone."

"She wasn't alone. She had you."

"You barely know me." She threw her hands up in exasperation. "What if I were some serial killer or baby snatcher?"

Max shrugged. "Sarah trusted you, and she is an excellent judge of character."

"Evidently not, since she hooked up with you." Alyssa's eyes widened, and her hand clapped over her mouth. "I'm sorry, Max, I didn't mean it."

"No, you did, but it's okay. You're right." He shook

his head and plopped down onto a barstool. "I don't know how to be a dad. I only know the single life. You should take Peyton before I make some colossal mistake and screw her up forever. I can pay for a nanny for her."

"Max, we've been through this. I can't take Peyton right now, and like it or not, you are her father, so you have to learn to take some responsibility. Look, I'll help out all I can, but you can't treat me like your babysitter and dump her on me while you go fulfill your"–her nose turned up in disgust as she uttered the last word–"urges."

"Fair enough," Max agreed. "I won't do it to you again."

She eyed him as if debating with herself if he would keep his promise. "Fine. I'll be over to pick up Peyton in the morning for church. Try to have her ready by 10:15."

"Church? I don't go to church."

"But Peyton does. Routines remember? And you don't have to come. You can stay here and do"–she waved her hand in the air–"whatever you do all day. When I get back, I'll teach you how to put Peyton down for a nap and we'll talk about the nanny situation."

"You mean I can't just take her with me?" He meant it as a joke to lighten the mood, but Alyssa merely crossed her arms again and raised an eyebrow at him. "Okay, okay. I'll call a nanny service tomorrow."

"You can't just get any nanny though. You have to get someone who will jibe with Peyton." She sighed. "Look, I don't have a final on Monday. Call and set up interviews for Monday, and I'll help you screen them. You can take a day off work, can't you?"

"I guess I'll have to. You know you're pretty cute when you're all riled up." He smirked at her, knowing the words would ruffle her feathers.

Sure enough, she stiffened and glared at him. "Don't even think about it. Some other woman's lipstick is still fresh on your neck, remember? Peyton's in bed. I'll show you how to do that tomorrow too, but for now I'm going to go study."

She whirled around and marched off, her shoulders pulled back and her head held high.

Max smiled at her retreating figure. It might take some time, but he was pretty sure he could win her over one day.

CHAPTER 6

*A*lyssa made her exit before he could say another word. She didn't want to chance him seeing the effect he had on her.

When she was safely in her car, she laid her head on the steering wheel. What was this feeling? Was this jealousy? She couldn't develop feelings for this man. Forget the part that he was her best friend's ex-lover, but he was also a complete player.

She had thought maybe Sarah had been exaggerating about his less than desirable qualities when she had met the man this morning. Though obviously clueless, he had seemed willing to do what it took to make sure his daughter was taken care of. It was almost… sweet. But then he had left her to go make out with some unknown woman. Worse yet, she was jealous.

Jealous! She should not be feeling jealousy. She should not be feeling anything for this man. He was a walking danger sign, neon lights and all.

Get ahold of yourself, Lyssa, you can't fall for this guy. The mantra played over and over in her head, but it couldn't seem to push the image of his arresting blue eyes out of her mind.

She was still trying to convince herself when she entered the apartment fifteen minutes later.

"How did it go?" Roxy asked. Roxy had been her roommate for the last few years and while the girls didn't see eye to eye on religion, they had enough other things in common that they became friends.

"Oh, um, fine, I guess."

"You guess, huh?" Roxy crooked an eyebrow and scrutinized Alyssa's face. "Let me guess, the man is handsome."

"What? Why would you say that?" Even as she protested, Alyssa could feel the heat burgeoning on her face.

"Your reaction for one. Plus, you came in all moony. I haven't seen you look like that in a long time."

There was truth to that. After a few bad relationships, Alyssa had pretty much sworn off men and focused completely on school. She couldn't even remember the last time she found a man attractive, until now. "Yeah," she sighed, "He's handsome, but he's also irritating and completely wrong for me."

"Sounds like you have it all figured out then," Roxy teased, as she turned her attention back to the television.

Alyssa had nothing figured out, but saying the words out loud had convinced her, at least a little. She headed to her room to spend some time in prayer and give the issue to God.

he next morning, she found herself waffling over what to wear for the first time in ages. It wasn't that she didn't normally take pride in her appearance, but today Maxwell would be seeing her, and she felt the need to dress even nicer.

Finally deciding on a hunter green shirt with a lace detail on the back and a black skirt, she dressed quickly. The green in the shirt brought out her eyes, causing the tiny gold flecks in them to sparkle. After a small dab of lip gloss for a little sheen, she headed out the door, Bible in hand.

Her heart began ramping up its acceleration as she pulled into Max's driveway, and her hands suddenly felt slicker than usual. What was going on with her? Why was she letting him affect her this way? She took several deep breaths on her way to the front door to try and calm her speeding heartbeat.

The door swung open just a minute after the doorbell chime had ended and Max stood on the other side in a pair of sweats and a white t-shirt that stretched across his well-formed chest.

"Good morning, you look beautiful," he said, swinging the door wider for her to enter.

She would take that as a compliment, but with his track record, he probably said that to every woman, even if they showed up in sweats. Still the look in his eyes sent a heat searing across her face as she stepped inside. "Thank you. You do as well."

His eyebrow raised at her as he glanced down at his casual dress, and her face flamed.

"I mean thank you." The smile on his face annoyed her. He was taking too much enjoyment in her discomfort. "Is Peyton ready?"

"Yes, she's in the kitchen finishing breakfast."

As Max led the way, Alyssa forced herself to focus on anything other than his physique. She didn't like him knowing he affected her.

Peyton sat at the table dressed in a pretty pink summery dress, but her hair was a mess. Tangles caused it to bunch together on one side, and on the other side, strands stuck out willy-nilly.

"Did you comb her hair at all?" Alyssa asked as she took in the disheveled appearance.

Max shrugged. "I wasn't sure how, and she didn't seem to want me to…" he trailed off.

"You can't let her make the rules. She's three. Come on Peyton." Grabbing the tiny hand, Alyssa propelled her down the hallway and to the bathroom. Once there, she grabbed the brush off the counter and slowly brought it through Peyton's thick hair.

"Ouch." Peyton's hand covered her head in an attempt to thwart Alyssa.

"Hold still. You can't go out looking like a ragamuffin. Your mother would beat me if I let you do that."

The mention of her mother calmed her down, and Peyton dropped her hands. Alyssa smiled up at Maxwell as she continued brushing. "See? That is how you win."

"I have a lot to learn," he said, shaking his head.

*M*ax smiled as he watched Alyssa finish cleaning Peyton up. She was cute when aggravated and even cuter when embarrassed. What was he thinking? He couldn't think about her like that. For one thing, she was a total Bible thumper, which would never work with his lifestyle, but he also needed her to

THE BILLIONAIRE'S SECRET | 49

help with Peyton, which meant he needed her to stay around, and he never let women stay more than one night. They got too clingy.

"Okay, I think we're ready," she said as she exited the bathroom.

Max smelled something sweet as she passed, some perfume that flooded his senses and sent his heart thumping. "Have fun." He meant it as a joke as he couldn't imagine church being fun, but she turned and smiled at him.

"We will."

Then they were gone, and the house was quiet. Max headed to the bathroom to take a shower before curling up on the couch to watch some sports. Football was over for the year, but he found a baseball game and settled back.

It didn't hold his interest though and after flipping the channels for a few minutes, he turned off the TV and wandered into the kitchen. He wasn't really hungry, but he made himself a couple of eggs, toast, and coffee to kill some time.

When the food was gone, he washed the plate and checked his watch. 11:15. He had no idea how long church services lasted. How weird that the house felt different without Peyton in it now. Normally, he would relish the solace of a quiet Sunday morning. Of course, he would usually be finishing a late breakfast with a date and then kissing her goodbye at the door right about now.

He moseyed down the hallway to Peyton's room and pushed open the door. Her few toys were scattered around, and he picked them up, placing them in the toy bin they had purchased. As he surveyed the room, he remembered the paint they had picked up. He could paint the walls while they're at church and have a surprise for Peyton when she returned. Plus, it would show Alyssa that he was trying.

After muscling the furniture to the center of the room, he grabbed the paint and rollers from the garage and headed back to the room.

The pink Alyssa picked wasn't too bright, and though he never thought he'd be painting his walls pink, he found he didn't mind it too much.

The doorbell rang before the job was finished. Placing the brush on the open can, he headed to the front door, checking his watch as he walked. 12:30, good to know.

"We're back," Alyssa said as he opened the door. "I see you've been busy."

"What?" He looked down and noticed paint splotches on his shirt. Good thing it wasn't one of his favorites. "Oh yeah, I thought I'd make myself useful while you guys were out. I didn't quite finish though."

"Hi, Max," Peyton said as she entered the house. "We went to church."

"Yeah, I know. Did you have fun?"

"Uh-huh."

"Did you manage to get any on the walls?" Alyssa's laugh was sweet, and the teasing glint in her eyes made her even more beautiful.

"I think I have done a good job so far." He crossed his arms and stuck out his chest. So what if he had a little paint on his shirt? He hadn't painted in years.

"Would you like some help?"

Max eyed her skirt and dress shirt. "You aren't really dressed to help."

"Well, I'm sure you have another old shirt and some sweats I could borrow, right?"

He had never let women wear his clothes, but the thought of Alyssa in them sent his heart racing. "Yeah, I can probably find something."

"Good. Is it okay if I lay Peyton down in your room since we're painting hers? She's already had lunch, and she was dozing off in the car."

Max quickly ran through a mental memory of his room. Was there anything out he wouldn't want Alyssa to see? Since he liked it clean and simple and was generally good at putting things away, he was almost positive it would be fine. "Sure, come on."

He led the way, trying to brush away the image of

Alyssa in his room for other reasons. As she laid Peyton in his king-sized bed, he grabbed a t-shirt and a pair of sweats from a drawer for her. "I'll let you get changed, and I'll go find another brush."

After scrounging in the garage for a few minutes, Max returned to Peyton's room, another brush in hand. Alyssa stood there, his clothes hanging off her lean frame but looking sexy nonetheless. "Here." He shoved the brush in her hand and turned back to the wall he was painting, trying to get the image of her out of his mind.

If she were any other woman, he doubted they would be getting much painting done, but Peyton was asleep in his bed, and there was something about decorating a kid's room that dampened the desire. Besides, Alyssa had been a help with Peyton, and he'd hate to lose that help.

The painting went much faster with her helping, and an hour later the room was done.

"You're a messy painter," she said as she smiled at him.

"What do you mean?" He looked at his side of the room. It didn't look any different than her side.

"You have paint on your face." Alyssa reached a hand out and touched his cheek, sending a tremor down his spine.

Max covered her hand with his as their eyes locked.

Kissing her would be a bad thing, but he couldn't seem to tell his body that.

"Max." Her voice was low and throaty with emotion. "I can't. I'm sorry."

Her hand slipped out from under his, leaving a cold and empty feeling where it had been.

"Aunt Lyssa?" Peyton's voice carried down the hallway and Alyssa hurried from the room to attend to her. Sighing, Max ran a hand through his dark hair in frustration before replacing the lid on the paint buckets and taking the brushes to the kitchen to wash them out.

As the water ran over them, sending swirls of pink paint down the drain, his mind returned to the previous moment when he had been alone with Alyssa. What was it with her? Why did she keep affecting him when he clearly knew how wrong they would be?

He was so lost in thought, he nearly dropped the brushes when Alyssa and Peyton entered a moment later. She had changed back into her church outfit, a sure sign she was leaving, and he couldn't help but feel disappointed.

"I have to go study, but I'll be back this evening to help put her to bed." Alyssa said. "Do you think you can manage not to screw up too badly in" —she checked her watch— "four hours?"

"Haha. I think we'll be fine."

"Good, I'll see you then." She bent down to Peyton's eye level. "Be good for Max, and I'll see you later, okay?"

"Okay, bye Aunt Lyssa."

"Bye Peyton. Bye Max."

He flashed a wave goodbye as he took the brushes out of the sink and laid them on a towel on the counter. "I have to make a few calls, Peyton. Do you want me to put on a movie for you?"

She scrunched her face as she thought about it. "No, I'll just play in my room."

"Okay, don't touch the walls though. They're still wet." As she wandered off down the hallway, he finished patting the brushes to dry them some. *Raising a kid isn't that hard. I can do this.*

He picked his phone up off the charger and googled a nanny agency. None were open on Sundays, but thankfully one had a call service that took his message and assured him they would send nanny candidates to his doorstep the next morning. His next call was to Justin to fill him in on the plan.

"A day's fine, but don't get dragged into this 'dad' thing. You don't want to get tied down yet."

"That's not happening," Max said, but as he hung up the phone, he wondered if being tied down would be so bad. Having Alyssa around had been rather nice, even though she was kind of a pain sometimes.

With nothing left to do and time on his hands, Max

collapsed on the inviting leather sofa and flicked on the television. Golf was on, but he was not a huge fan. News and reruns didn't grab his attention either. Another click landed him on some movie channel. He left it there for lack of something better, but soon found his attention focused on it.

The movie followed a philandering man who suddenly woke up with a wife and kids and found himself a poor preacher rather than the rich business man he was at the beginning. At first the man was angry and wanted to get back to his original life, but as the movie progressed, the man found a fulfillment with his wife and kids that he never had with his job, and he wanted to stay in the new life.

The similarities were not lost on Max, and he leaned forward, engrossed in the story.

"What are you doing?"

He jumped at the sound of Peyton's voice. How had he missed her entering the room? She was like a tiny ninja. "I'm watching a movie," he said patting the couch beside him. "Do you want to finish it with me?"

Peyton pursed her little lips, but climbed up beside him. Max found himself wishing there was more left in the movie as the feeling of Peyton sitting beside him was enjoyable.

"Max, do you want to color with me?" Peyton asked, when the movie ended.

Max couldn't remember the last time he colored or the last time he thought it sounded fun, but he agreed and joined Peyton at the dining room table. She handed him a book filled with dogs, and he picked up a crayon.

As his crayon moved over the paper, he wondered if he could be happy like this. Could he get used to a life with Peyton in it full-time?

"You like coloring?" she asked.

"I like coloring with you," he said, smiling.

After they finished, she asked him to read her a book and play dolls with her. Though completely out of his comfort zone, he stretched out on the floor and held one of her dolls while she created a fantastical story about them. He caught most of it, but a few of her words were still hard to understand.

At six on the button, the doorbell chimed. Alyssa stood on the other side, holding bags of grocery food. "I looked in your fridge last night and noticed you didn't have a lot of fresh ingredients. I thought I could bring some over and cook dinner."

Max had never let a woman use his kitchen, but he stepped back, allowing Alyssa to enter. She handed him a few bags and, after shutting the door, he followed her into the kitchen.

"Aunt Lyssa. We're playing dolls, wanna play?"

"Dolls, huh?" She raised an eyebrow at Max as she set the bags on the counter. He shrugged. "I would, sweetie, but I'm going to make us some dinner. How does spaghetti sound?"

"Yay, pasgetti." Peyton ran off with her doll, leaving the two of them alone in the kitchen.

"Do you know how to make it?" she asked Max. "It's a kid staple, so you should learn if not."

"I think I can handle boiling some water," he said as he grabbed the large pot from the bottom cabinet. He filled it with water and placed it on the stove.

"Good, though there's a little more to it than that." She began pulling out groceries and putting them away in his fridge and his pantry.

He watched her, unsure of what else to do. Part of him wanted to tell her to stop, that this was his kitchen, but the other part of him enjoyed watching her shuffle ingredients around, as if she'd cooked here a million times.

When the water began to boil, she handed him the spaghetti strands and then began opening up cupboards.

"What are you looking for?"

"A skillet to brown the meat."

He reached into the bottom cupboard and pulled one out. Their gazes locked as he handed it to her. The moment drug out until she shook her head as if mentally breaking the connection.

"Thank you. Can you get me the hamburger meat?" She pointed to a package of ground beef on the counter.

He handed it to her and watched as she began browning the meat.

"Why don't you finish the salad?"

Max followed her finger to a large bowl filled with greens. A tomato sat on a cutting board next to it. Grabbing the knife, he made short work of the tomato and added the chunks to the salad.

"Where are your paper plates?" Alyssa asked a few minutes later, poking her head out of the pantry. "I wanted to use them for the salads."

"I don't have any. The plates are in the cupboard closest to the sink." He pointed in the direction as he grabbed parmesan cheese from the fridge.

Alyssa shook her head, but grabbed the plates and set them down on the counter. Max loaded each up with a scoop of spaghetti and salad, and the two carried the plates to the table.

"Peyton? Dinner's ready."

At Alyssa's words, Peyton scurried into the living room and climbed up in her chair.

As he sat down, Max noticed Peyton's hands folded together. Alyssa struck a similar pose, and Max was left staring at his plate uncomfortably as the two prayed over theirs.

"You don't pray?" Alyssa asked as she finished her prayer.

"No, I don't believe in God, so, why would I?"

"You'll still take me to church though, won't you, Max?" Peyton's voice was small and pulled on Max's heart.

He opened his mouth to speak, but before he could, Alyssa jumped in. "I'll come get you Peyton, okay?"

Peyton nodded and took a bite of her spaghetti. Max looked from one to the other, deciding this was a perfect arrangement. He could stay out late on Saturdays and Alyssa could take Peyton to church while he slept in the next morning. Now, he just needed to find someone who could watch her on Saturday nights.

After dinner, Alyssa helped him clear the table and put away the leftover spaghetti. "I'm going to put Peyton down. Do you want to come watch how it should be done?"

There was no condescension in her words this time. Only sincerity. "Sure, why not?"

Alyssa frowned at his flippant attitude, but turned to Peyton. "Peyton, honey, it's time for bed. Grab your bear."

Without a word of protest, Peyton grabbed her bear and headed down the hall to the room they had fixed up for her. As Alyssa grabbed pajamas for Peyton and helped her change, Max touched the walls. The paint had dried, so he scooted the toddler bed back to the wall, smoothing out the pink Minnie Mouse bedspread before retreating to the doorway to watch. As there was no chair in the room, Peyton and Alyssa sat on the bed and Alyssa read one of the books they had picked up yesterday. Alyssa's voice was soft and soothing as she read, and Max crossed his arms. He couldn't imagine doing this routine himself.

When the book was finished, Peyton crawled under the covers and Alyssa sat on the floor beside her. "Lord, thank you for Max and for the blessings you have bestowed upon him that allow him to watch Peyton. Please heal Sarah and bring her back to us and help Peyton get adjusted to this new life until that happens. Help us keep our eyes on you. In your name, amen."

The mention of his name in the prayer surprised him.

"Amen," Peyton echoed. "Thank you, Aunt Lyssa. Thank you, Max." Peyton's voice was heavy with sleep as she pulled her bear closer to her. Alyssa leaned down and placed a kiss on her forehead before standing.

Max stepped out of the way as Alyssa approached the doorframe and pulled the door closed behind her. "Thank you for coming here today and helping me with Peyton." His gaze locked on hers. She was beautiful, and though he knew it would never work, that knowledge didn't stop his desire.

"You're welcome," she said, clearing her throat and looking away. "I promised Sarah I would help."

Right, Sarah. Alyssa was only here because of Sarah.

He should remember that, and he should be thinking more about Sarah. After all, he needed her to get better or else he'd be watching Peyton forever, but Alyssa kept appearing in his mind.

"Did you call the nanny agency?" Her eyes were still averted as she asked the question.

"Yes, they said they'd send the candidates starting at ten a.m."

"Great, I'll see you then."

CHAPTER 7

*A*lyssa checked her outfit in the mirror one more time before grabbing her keys. She shouldn't care what she was wearing, but there was some unknown need to make a good impression on Max. The image of their locked gaze and the texture of his cheek against her hand had played through her mind the previous night. She had wanted him to kiss her. Why had she said no?

Yes, there was Sarah to consider, but Sarah had told her she was over Max. If Alyssa was honest, it had more to do with his lack of faith and his lifestyle.

Her freshman year of college, a junior had approached her. He was popular and appeared nice, but it turned out he only went after freshmen to score. When she refused to sleep with him, he had dropped her like a hot potato. Though she knew it was nothing she had done, it still stung, and it had affected her trust of men in the next few relationships.

With Max's past, she knew getting tangled up with him would probably lead to heartbreak, but her heart didn't seem to want to take her brain's advice.

Her traitorous heart began its steady ascent as she pulled into Max's driveway and parked the car. Why did he affect her this way? She took a deep breath on her way to the door in hopes of calming the erratic beating of her heart before pressing the doorbell.

A minute later, Max opened the door wearing cargo shorts and a blue button-down shirt that highlighted the matching color in his eyes. With the top two buttons undone, a hint of his muscular chest appeared. Heat seared across Alyssa's cheeks as she forced her gaze up to his face, but not fast enough. A playful smirk crossed Max's lips.

"Come on in. We have half an hour. Would you like coffee?"

"Tea." Her voice was raspy as it fought to escape past the emotions lodged in her throat. She cleared it and tried again. "Do you have any tea?"

He flicked his head in a "follow me" gesture and led the way into the kitchen. *Get ahold of yourself Alyssa. You're acting like a school girl.*

Peyton sat coloring at the table as they entered, and hoping to regain her composure, Alyssa joined her while

Max set the kettle on the stove and rummaged in the pantry for tea.

When the kettle whistled moments later, he placed a steaming mug in front of her before pulling out a chair and sitting, a similar cup of coffee in his hand.

"You color?" Alyssa couldn't hide the surprise in her voice as he reached for a crayon.

"Yeah, Peyton and I colored last night before you came back. Evidently, I'm a natural." He turned the book around for her to see the image, and the attention to detail was amazing. He had used shading and highlighting to bring the images to life.

"Did you study art?"

"Well, I am in advertising, so I've learned a few things along the way." The crooked smile he flashed sent her heart dancing again, and she dropped her eyes to her mug to hide the effect.

The doorbell rang as Alyssa took her last sip of tea. "Here we go," she said, pushing back from the table.

"Why don't you and Peyton sit in the living room, and I'll bring in the first one?" Max was heading down the hallway as he finished the question.

Alyssa took Peyton's hand and led her to the plush couch. "Okay, Miss Peyton, we will interview women to watch you while Max is at work. You be sure and tell us the ones you like and the ones you don't, okay?"

"Okay." Peyton's eyes displayed a smidgen of fear, but she hugged her bear and nodded.

Max returned a moment later with a blond woman trailing behind him. A tight bun topped her hair, and a flawlessly pressed skirt and shirt hugged her curves. A string of pearls hung around her neck. She appeared dressed more for a date than interviewing for a nanny position.

"Alyssa, Peyton, this is Claire. She has nannied for several families in the area."

As Claire glanced Alyssa's direction, it was obvious that she found her competition and was sizing her up. Alyssa shifted in her seat as she tried to keep an open mind. She wasn't dating Max after all.

"Yes, my last family was the Mayor's family. Their children outgrew the need for a nanny which is why I am even available. I have an impeccable list of references."

Max waved the two crisp white sheets of paper as evidence and nodded at Alyssa to take the lead.

"Claire, describe a typical day with Peyton under your charge."

Like a machine, Claire recited the passé statements. "I'll feed her, play with her, read to her, etc.," but the words rang hollow to Alyssa's ears. While she had no doubt the woman *could* watch Peyton, she couldn't see any bond of trust forming.

"Thank you, we'll be in touch."

Claire blinked at Alyssa before turning to Max for confirmation. She must have thought her references alone would get her hired on the spot, but Max took Alyssa's lead and walked the woman out.

"What was wrong with her?" he asked when he returned.

Alyssa smiled and turned to Peyton. "You want to tell him?"

"Too stiff," Peyton said, shaking her head.

A chuckle bubbled out of Max's lips. "Yeah, I guess she was, wasn't she?"

The following three women were like Claire, and Peyton negated each one with the same two words, but she brightened when Max returned with the next candidate, an older woman with more silver than brown left in her hair. She wore a pair of glasses that slid down her nose, causing her to keep pushing them up, and she was plump like a teddy bear but nicely dressed. Alyssa wondered if Peyton's attraction to her stemmed from the fact she had no grandmother, at least not on Sarah's side.

"Well, aren't you a dearie?" The woman's voice held the hint of an old English accent as she smiled at Peyton.

"This is Helen. Helen, this is Alyssa and Peyton." After making the introduction, Max sat beside Alyssa on the couch. She flashed him a quick glance. It was the first time he had sat next to her. For the other interviews, he had perched on the other couch, but she wasn't complaining.

"Now, I know I'm a bit older than the other women you've interviewed, but don't let my age fool you. I'm a grandmum to six babes and I can keep up with them."

"I have no doubt," Alyssa said with a laugh. "Well, why don't you tell us how Peyton would spend her day."

"I believe in starting with a healthy breakfast and quiet time where we will either read or do crafts. Then I prefer to go outdoors. Fresh air is good for children, you know. Lunch will follow and a nap if she still takes one. If the weather is nice, we will read and go outside again. Art projects are my passion, so we'll do many of them, and I'd teach her how to cook and sew. It is important that children learn to do things on their own."

Alyssa sneaked a peek at Peyton, but even those words didn't strike the smile from her face. With a slight nudge, she motioned Max to look at Peyton who was still staring at Helen with bright eyes and an open expression.

"Peyton is pleased, so I guess I am too." He glanced at Alyssa who nodded back.

"Can I say you two make the cutest couple? The love is abundant in this house." Helen smiled at Max and Alyssa.

"Oh, no, we're not a couple…" Alyssa began.

"We're not together…" Max said at the same time.

Peyton giggled, and Helen winked at her. "My mistake. You appear so in sync."

A blush spread across Alyssa's face as Max cleared his throat. "Yes, Alyssa has been a great help, and I feel you'd be wonderful for Peyton. Can you start tomorrow?"

"I can. Seven o'clock?"

"That will be fine." Max rose from the couch and shook her hand.

Alyssa stood beside him and shook Helen's hand next, trying not to smile as Helen winked at her. If Helen saw something between the two of them, could there be something there?

"I like her," Peyton said as Max walked Helen out.

"Me too." Alyssa glanced at her watch, but it was barely noon. Should she stay or should she go?

"Well, I don't know about you, but I'm hungry," Max said as he re-entered the room. "What do you say we grab lunch to celebrate?"

"Yes, lunch." Peyton clapped her hands.

"Did you get a bigger car yet or should we take mine?" Alyssa asked.

"No, they delivered the Malibu yesterday, and I have the car seat in the back, though you should make sure I got it in right."

Alyssa tilted her head at him, surprised. "Okay, let's go then."

After a quick check of the car seat, she nodded her approval and helped strap Peyton in before climbing in the passenger side. "It's nice," she said, feeling the leather sets.

"Hmm, yeah, it's not bad."

She turned shocked eyes on him. "Do you mean you didn't test drive it when you bought it?"

He shrugged. "Nope, I told the salesman to get me the safest car with those hook thingies."

Alyssa shook her head as he started the engine. Their lives were so different.

A few minutes later, they arrived in the parking lot of an upscale restaurant. Images of Peyton fussing or crying and annoying the wait staff filled her mind. "You want to take Peyton in here?" Alyssa couldn't keep the incredulity out of her voice. "It is near her naptime."

"And?" The subtlety of her hint was lost on him.

"Sometimes even well-behaved children have a hard time being quiet when they are hungry and tired."

"I'm sure it will be fine."

The edge in his tone told her he hadn't taken her advice the way she meant it. Alyssa shrugged, not wanting to argue with him, and opened her door. After he rescued Peyton from the backseat, they headed into the restaurant.

A woman in a starched white shirt and spotless black pants greeted them. "Welcome. How many?"

"Three," Max said, taking charge.

"Will you need a high chair?" the woman asked, nodding at Peyton.

"Yes." Alyssa jumped in before Max could say no. He hadn't been out to eat with Peyton yet, but she knew if the girl wasn't locked down, a bumpy meal was ahead.

"Okay, I guess yes."

"Perfect, it will be about fifteen minutes. Can I get a name?"

Max left his name as Peyton tugged on his pant leg.

"Fifteen minutes? But I'm hungry now."

Alyssa pressed her lips together and raised her eyebrows at him. This was what she had feared. Peyton's voice was dripping with whine.

"Don't worry, Peyton, it rarely takes as long as they say."

His luck held this time as the hostess called his name just a few minutes later. As she led them to the table, Alyssa noticed an extra sway in her hips and the meaningful look she flashed at Max as she seated them. Did women everywhere come onto him all the time?

Max, to his credit, either didn't notice or ignored the gesture as he picked Peyton up and deposited her in the high chair.

"Don't forget to strap it."

He looked at Alyssa as if she had spoken in a foreign language.

"The high chair strap. Trust me, you want to fasten it."

"Is she Houdini or something?" he asked, snapping the strap together before taking his seat.

Alyssa laughed. "You don't understand. Once, she stood up in the high chair before we could catch her and she snagged the arm of a waiter passing by with a tray full of food. Burgers and fries went flying everywhere."

Max's eyes widened in alarm, and he checked the strap one more time. "That can't happen here. We could never return."

"You'll learn that with little kids, these places may need to wait for dates or special occasions." Alyssa's face flamed as the mention of dates. Would he think she was asking him out or hinting for him to ask her out?

"What about you?" he asked.

"What about me what?"

"Do you want kids one day?"

Alyssa glanced at Peyton who was coloring on the paper the hostess had provided. "Yes, I'd like a family with at least three kids."

"I never thought I wanted kids, but Peyton is cool, and there's something about her that warms my heart."

The tone in his voice as he spoke of Peyton and the look in his eyes as he glanced at her coloring warmed Alyssa's heart, but she couldn't say those thoughts out loud. "It's not all unicorns and rainbows though." Alyssa didn't want to scare him, but she would be remiss if she didn't prepare him for the other side. "There will be tantrums and sicknesses and you can't just leave the house on a whim."

"I'm hungry," Peyton said, interrupting their conversation. Her voice was an octave louder than necessary. She complemented her whine with banging her small hands on the table and throwing the crayons.

"Peyton, stop!" Max's voice was quiet and terse, and he glanced around at the other patrons.

"It's okay, Max. She's just hungry," Alyssa said. "For these times, I always bring something with me." She dug in her purse for a moment before pulling out a small square cube.

"What's that?" Max asked as she handed it to Peyton.

"It's a fidget cube. The buttons push in and out. It's smart to always have something on you to keep Peyton entertained."

Max tilted his head at her. "How did you learn all this?"

"From watching Sarah. She is an amazing mother."

Peyton looked up from the dice. "I miss mommy."

"I know, baby, but she's trying to get better."

The waitress returned then, placing a tray of bread in the middle of the table. Max grabbed a piece, but he didn't eat it. Instead, he rolled it in his hand as if something was on his mind. "How long have you known Sarah?"

"About three years, I guess. I met her after Peyton was born. I offered to rent a place with her, but she was determined to do it all on her own. Since we hit it off though, she let me come around and help with Peyton."

"I'm sorry I missed those days." His soft voice pulled at Alyssa's heart.

She tore a piece of bread for herself, debating if she should ask the question rattling around in her head. "What happened with you and Sarah? I mean, I know how it ended, but why?"

Max took a bite of his bread and glanced at Peyton before answering. "I think I wasn't prepared. I wasn't ready to be with just one woman, but I loved Sarah. I would have done anything for her, and I'd like to think I would have settled down if I'd known about Peyton."

Their heavy discussion was broken when the waitress returned again to take their order. The rest of the lunch conversation was lighter, but Alyssa couldn't help looking at Max a little differently. Sarah must not have known how he felt about her because she rarely spoke of him, and when she did, it was always about his philandering. Alyssa was now seeing a different side of him, and it was one she could learn to like.

CHAPTER 8

When the alarm went off the next morning, Max hit the buzzer and replayed the previous day in his mind.

After lunch, Alyssa had excused herself to go study. Max had been left with Peyton again, and after an hour blowing bubbles and another coloring, she had become cranky and whiny. Max had sat her in front of the television and suffered through cartoons with her until bedtime.

Then, he hadn't done her bedtime routine correctly, and she had teared up, crying for Sarah. Needless to say, after a good morning, his day had quickly deteriorated, leaving him wondering if he could raise Peyton on his own.

With a sigh, he pushed himself out of bed and into

his bathroom. After a quick shower, he donned a blue chambray shirt and khaki slacks. The hall was silent as he made his way to the kitchen, but he checked Peyton's room just to be sure.

She was still sleeping, her hair fanning out around her. He smiled as he shut the door quietly behind him and continued down the hallway. As hard as last night was, she looked like an angel when she slept.

Once in the kitchen, he readied the coffee pot and pressed the button to start it percolating. Then he began preparing his protein waffle for breakfast. He had just finished the last bite and was rinsing the plate in the sink when the doorbell rang.

Hoping it wouldn't wake Peyton, he hurried to open it. Helen stood on the other side, her arms laden with bags.

"What is all this?" he asked as he grabbed a few bags from her, freeing her arms.

"Crafts and games for Peyton. I hope you'll forgive me, but I didn't see many when I was here yesterday. I had a ton sitting around my house."

"That's fine, just try not to make a huge mess." In his mind, he could see paint and markers all over his floors and walls. So far, Peyton had kept the house clean and most of the mess in her room, but he feared with all these crafts that it would trickle into his space. He set the bags down on the dining table as they entered the kitchen area.

"I always clean up whatever mess I might make, Mr. Banks."

She had pulled her shoulders back, and he knew he had ruffled her feathers, but he didn't have much time to apologize. He was running late for work.

"Glad to hear it," he said, grabbing his coffee mug and his satchel. "I'll be home after work."

"Mr. Banks," she called after him, but he didn't turn around. He felt a little bad when he realized he had forgotten to show her around and she was probably just asking for directions, but she seemed like a smart lady, and he was sure she would figure it out.

He slid into the BMW, the leather seat fitting like an old, comfortable glove, perfectly molded to his shape. *Ah, this is so much better.* The Malibu drove well, but it just didn't hold a candle to his BMW.

"Welcome back, man," Justin said as Max entered the office. He held up his hand for a high five, and Max slapped it back. It was good to be back at work where he felt like a grownup again.

"I've only been gone one day." He picked up the messages on his desk left by his assistant from the previous day and rifled through them.

"Yeah, but Maxwell Banks never misses work. What's going on with you man?"

Max shook his head. "I'm trying to get used to having a toddler in my house. I thought it would be easy, and sometimes it is, but then she cries and I don't know how to handle it."

"Dude, I know Sarah didn't have a family, but are you sure you want to keep this kid? Couldn't you put her in foster care?"

Max glanced up at Justin. Though the thought had crossed his mind a few times, he would never say it out loud. "I'm not going to do that. It's not the way I would have wanted it, but I'm going to take responsibility for my actions."

"Sure man, that's admirable, but it's really going to cramp your style."

Max knew that as well, but he was nearing thirty, so maybe changing his style wouldn't be such a bad thing. "I better get to returning these calls." He waved the stack at Justin for emphasis.

"Sure, man, lunch though?"

"Yeah, lunch sounds good."

Shaking his head, Max picked up the first message and the phone.

"*H*ey, man, you ready for lunch?"

Max glanced up at Justin and down at

his watch. Four hours had passed already? "Yeah, give me one second. Where are you thinking?"

"We haven't been to Hooters in a while."

Max nodded. Though he'd never drink while at work, taking in the view of the wait staff would be a welcome relief.

Twenty minutes later, the two were at a table admiring the tight tops and short shorts as the women bustled back and forth.

"We should go out after work," Justin suggested, his eyes following a busty blond. "Today is busy, and I could sure use a drink. You have someone to watch the kid, right?"

"Yeah, I have a nanny now. I never knew the cost to raise a kid, but my wallet has certainly taken a hit since Friday night." Max took a sip of his tea as he checked out a passing brunette. *Pretty, but not as pretty as Alyssa.* He coughed on his tea a little as he realized he was comparing these women to the one woman he should stay away from.

"You all right?" Justin asked.

"Yeah." Max wondered if he really was though. He couldn't remember the last time a woman kept appearing in his head like Alyssa did.

The waitress appeared a few moments later, and after taking their order, she laid a napkin down in front of Max and winked at him. "For later," she said before sashaying away.

Max picked up the napkin to see a name and number scrawled across it.

"What is it?" Justin asked, leaning across the table to try to catch a glance.

"Her number," Max said. He folded the napkin and shoved it in his pocket though he wasn't sure he had any intention of using it.

"You sly dog. Well, I guess you have your weekend planned now." Justin winked at him as he picked up his glass and took another swig.

Max nodded, but suddenly he couldn't wait to get out of the restaurant.

❦

"*H*ey, we're heading out to Charlie's for a drink. You coming?" Justin stood in Max's office doorway tapping the face of his watch.

"Yeah, let me call the nanny." Max picked up his work phone and dialed his home number. He had given Helen the green light to answer phone calls while he was at work, so he hoped she followed through.

"Hello?"

"Helen, It's Max. Can you stay with Peyton a little longer tonight? I uh need to catch up on some work." He had no idea why the lie tumbled out instead of the truth, but there was not much he could do about it now.

"Sure, do you have a time estimate or should I plan on putting her to bed?" Though Helen's words were friendly, he could hear something in her tone.

"Um, I'm not sure. It should only be a few hours."

"Okay, then. I'll let her know."

The phone clicked without a goodbye, and Max sighed. He would have to do something nice for her. He couldn't afford to lose a nanny Peyton liked.

"All right, let's go."

"Awesome. I'll meet you there."

*C*harlie's was just getting busy when they arrived. After scanning the room, Justin waved to a few other people from work and the two headed that direction.

"Maxwell, we didn't expect to see you. Justin told us about your kid issue," Jake, one of their sales reps said, from the back of the booth.

"It's not really an issue," Max said, sliding in beside Rhea, one of their receptionists. "Peyton is pretty cool."

The others nodded, but their faces registered their disbelief. He couldn't blame them. He would have had the same expression a few days ago.

"Two beers please," Justin said when the waitress stopped by, and a few minutes later, the pale amber liquid was set in front of Max.

He took a swig as he listened to the conversation of the surrounding group. As the liquid worked its magic, he found himself thinking less of Peyton and Alyssa and more of nights out like this. That was, until his phone rang.

Grabbing it from his pocket and shooting apologetic looks at the rest of the crowd, he stood up as he punched the answer button and headed for the outside door where it was quieter.

"Hello?" He had to jam a finger in his opposite ear until he reached the front entrance in order to hear the voice on the other end.

"Maxwell? Where are you?"

The voice threw him for a moment as the last time he heard his name used with such vitriol was when he was in trouble with his mother.

"Alyssa?"

"Yes, it's Alyssa. Care to guess where I'm at? I'll tell you. I'm at your house, consoling your daughter because she thought yet another person was abandoning her when you didn't come home today."

"I told Helen I had to work late," Max said, the lie spilling from his lips before he could stop it.

"Yes, and that would have been fine except you

aren't at work. Helen tried your office before calling me. You forgot to give her your cell phone number, but thankfully you left mine up on the fridge."

"Is Peyton okay?" Max glanced at his watch. He had only been out an extra two hours, but that must seem a lifetime to a three-year-old.

"She is now that I'm here, but Max you can't do this to her." Her voice softened, "She just lost her mother. She can't afford to lose you too."

"I'll be right there." Max hung up the phone and stepped back into the noisy restaurant. It wouldn't be right to leave without at least telling Justin what had happened.

"What's up, Max?" Justin asked as he approached the table. "Where did you go?"

"Sorry, that was Alyssa. Evidently Peyton had a scare. I have to go." He reached into his wallet and pulled out a twenty. "This should cover my drinks. I'll see you tomorrow." Without waiting for the protest he knew would come, he turned and walked out of the bar.

Though the drive only took him fifteen minutes, he felt even worse when he arrived home and saw Peyton curled up on Alyssa's lap in the living room.

Alyssa held a finger to her lips, telling him to be quiet. With a small sigh, he sat beside her on the couch.

"I messed up big time, didn't I?" he whispered to her.

Her eyes stared into his. "It's a big change, having a kid in your life, but you have to think about her now and not so much about yourself."

"I'm trying, but I guess I still have a lot to learn. Thank you for coming though."

"Of course. I'll always be here for Peyton."

Her words struck his heart. She would be there for Peyton, but would she ever be there for him? Probably not, if he kept messing up.

"Shall we lay her down?" Max whispered.

Alyssa nodded and shifted Peyton slightly in her arms, so Max could reach down and scoop Peyton up. Her head flopped onto his chest, but her eyes remained closed as he carried her down the hallway, Alyssa a step behind.

Peyton mumbled softly in her sleep as Max laid her in the bed. He touched her forehead and smoothed her hair back. He hated that he hurt her even though he hadn't meant to.

Alyssa stood just outside the room as he closed the door.

"Thank you for coming. Again, I'm so sorry."

"You're welcome, but I have to get back to studying now."

"What are you studying?"

"Psychology. I want to be a therapist or a counselor. I think."

A light chuckle crossed her lips as she said the last two words, and he wondered why. She would make an excellent counselor; he found himself wanting to talk to her about anything and everything, something very unusual for him. Usually, he said just what he had to do to get the woman home with him and in his bed and then he let his body do the rest of the talking. While he couldn't deny he wouldn't love to share his bed with Alyssa, he was also interested in her mind.

"I think you would make an excellent counselor. I know you've really helped me." He reached out and grabbed her hand.

"Max, I... I'll come check on Peyton later in the week." She extricated her hand and turned to leave.

"Wait, when is your last final?" he asked, stopping her.

"Thursday, why?"

"Can I take you to lunch on Friday? As a thank you and to celebrate the end of your finals," he added hastily, hoping it would feel less like a date to her that way and she would say yes.

Her eyes stared into his. They were a deep emerald like pine trees, and he could get lost in them easily.

"Just lunch?" she asked.

"Just lunch, and you can tell me more things I need to know to keep Peyton happy. I'll be a sponge soaking up all your advice. Promise."

A tiny smile flicked across her mouth at his analogy. "Okay, just lunch. Shall I meet you at your office at noon?"

"That would be wonderful," Max said and pulled a business card out of his wallet for her. He almost couldn't believe he had agreed to her coming to his office; he would never have done that in the past, but Alyssa was different.

She took the card, nodding at him as she left. It was not the reaction he had been hoping for, but she had agreed and that meant the door was at least open a crack. He would find a way to show her he was changing.

CHAPTER 9

*P*eyton was still sleeping when Helen arrived the next morning. Though tempted to be late to work to talk to her, Max still had a lot on his plate to catch up on after taking Monday off.

"I owe you an apology, Helen," Max said as she entered the kitchen. "I wasn't working late last night. I went out with friends. I'm not sure why I didn't tell you the truth, but I promise I will in the future."

Helen tilted her head, regarding him with her experienced eyes. "I can tell you are trying, Max, but it is important that I can reach you at all times."

He nodded. "I've written down my cell number for you." He slid the paper across the counter to her. "I'll be home no later than 6:30 tonight, I promise."

"Max, you're back." Peyton's voice broke into the conversation. She had entered the kitchen silently again.

"I was home last night, Peyton, and I'm sorry I worried you. I'm not going anywhere." He leaned down and hugged her.

"Okay. Look what Helen and I did." Her excitement was barely contained as she bounced up and down on her toes. Any hurt from yesterday appeared to have been forgiven and forgotten. Grabbing his hand, she pulled him into the dining room. "We painted my high fives."

On a white canvas board were two perfect hand prints in pink and purple. Peyton's name was spelled out across the top and the year was at the bottom. Those small hand prints tugged on Maxwell's heart. Suddenly, he realized all the time he missed with Peyton—time when her hands were even smaller—and it hurt. He had never gotten to hold her as a baby or watch her take her first steps. He had no idea what her first word was. Though this realization rocked him, he pasted a smile on his face to mask his emotions.

"It's beautiful, Peyton. We must hang it somewhere special."

"There will be more years in the future," Helen said, coming up beside him. "You may have missed the beginning, but you'll have plenty more if you are paying attention."

Max stared at her with wide eyes. How had she read his mind?

"Besides, I believe there will be more children in your future."

The words were so quiet, he wasn't sure he even heard her right, and before he could ask her to repeat them, she had scooted away and was rummaging in her bag.

"*W*hat happened last night?" Justin asked, plopping down in the seat across from Maxwell.

"I scared Peyton." Max said, turning on his computer for the day. "She is still adjusting to not having Sarah, and she feared I was abandoning her."

"Dude, are you sure you want to keep doing this?"

"I'm not shipping her off to foster care. I'll figure it out."

Justin held his hands in a defensive posture as he stood. "Hey man, I'm just trying to look out for you."

Max sighed as Justin left the office. He doubted Justin would ever fully understand.

*A*t six pm, Max turned off his computer and headed home. He still had work to catch up on, but he had promised Helen he would come straight home.

Peyton greeted him at the door. "Max, I drew a picture." She tugged his hand, pulling him down the hallway. Max smiled at her exuberance. There was something contagious about her positive attitude.

"I drew us." She pointed proudly to a white picture with four colorful blobs. "There's me and there's you. There's Aunt Lyssa and there's Helen."

Max noticed she hadn't drawn Sarah, but he didn't point it out to her in fear of making her cry again. "That's beautiful, Peyton. Shall we hang it on the fridge?" He glanced over at his stainless-steel fridge. It had always been completely bare, just the way he liked it. Alyssa's card was the only thing on it, and it was small enough not to grab much attention, but he wanted Peyton to understand he was proud of her. Swallowing his fear of clutter, he grabbed a piece of tape to post it in the middle of the fridge.

"You'll be glad you did." Helen patted him on the shoulder, and Max wondered again how she seemed to always know his thoughts. "I'll see you tomorrow. There's dinner in the oven which should be ready"—she held up her finger and a timer dinged — "now!"

As Helen said goodbye to Peyton, Max grabbed plates and set the table. Helen had prepared a cheesy casserole which he scooped onto each plate. He added left-over salad and helped Peyton up into her chair.

"Aren't you going to pray?" she asked as he picked up his fork.

"Why don't you do it?"

She bowed her head and closed her eyes. "Dear God, thank you for food and Max and Helen and Aunt Lyssa. Help Mommy get better. Amen."

It was a sweet prayer, and though Max wasn't the praying kind, the words resonated with him. What must that kind of faith be like?

After dinner, Peyton watched television while he cleaned up. Then he joined her in the living room.

"Can I sit on your lap?" she asked as he plopped down on the couch.

Max hesitated. He had never been one to show too much affection; he rarely cuddled with women, but the angelic look on her face caused him to nod. She climbed up in his lap and curled against his chest.

Her hair smelled sweet like strawberries, and though it was an added weight, he didn't mind and curled his arms around her.

"Okay, bedtime," he said when the show ended.

"Do I have to?" she whined.

"Yes, you have to. Come on."

Begrudgingly, she followed him to her room, her bare feet plopping on the hardwood floor with her exaggerated steps. Max pulled out jammies and helped her change before helping her into bed.

"Read this one," she said, handing him a book with Elmo on the cover.

Max opened the book and read. When he finished, Peyton's eyes started to close, but before he could get away, she opened them and focused on him.

"Will you pray with me?"

The question caught him off guard as he tucked her into her bed. "Um, I'm not sure how, Peyton."

"It's easy. Just close your eyes and thank God. You can ask him for things too, but not too many."

Max smiled at her innocence. "Okay, I'll try." He closed his eyes and cleared his throat. "God? I don't know if you recognize me, but I'm praying for Peyton. Thank you for letting me meet her and help her to be happy and sleep well. Um, amen?"

Peyton giggled. "See, was that so hard?"

"No, I guess not," Max said, enjoying the smile on her face. "Now get some sleep. You have another fun day tomorrow."

"Okay, night Max."

"Good night, Peyton."

He touched her forehead lightly before standing and exiting the room.

As he undressed for bed that night, he pondered his life. He had thought he was happy, spending his weeks alone and his weekends with beautiful women, but in the last few days, something had shifted. He wondered if his weekend flings were because he was looking for something more but not finding it.

"*H*ey, man, we're going out again tonight. You coming?" Justin stood in his office doorway, looking hopeful.

"No, not tonight. Peyton and I have a movie date planned."

Justin entered the office and sat in one of the open chairs. "What's going on with you, man? You seem different."

After taking a deep breath, Max replied. "I think I am different. Peyton is amazing, and I'm enjoying being a dad, and then there's Alyssa."

"Wait, who's Alyssa?"

"Sarah's friend, the one helping me with Peyton. She's beautiful and smart and spirited." A smile stretched across his face as he spoke about her.

"Dude, are you falling for her?" Justin's head

dropped forward as his left eyebrow went up.

"Maybe." Max glanced at Justin before returning his attention to the computer. He had to finish one more report before he would feel comfortable leaving for the day. "I mean I'm looking forward to seeing her again. We're having lunch tomorrow."

Justin let out a low whistle. "She better be something special if she's taking Maxwell Banks off the market."

Off the market? Was she taking him off the market? He certainly didn't have the same desire to date other women he used to, but was he ready to be a one-woman man?

"Peyton was wonderful today," Helen said, greeting him at the door. "Tomorrow is your lunch with Alyssa, right?"

Max didn't know what it was about Helen. He had only known her a week but was comfortable sharing his life with her. "Yes, she's meeting me at the office tomorrow and going to lunch. Can I ask you something? It's about Alyssa. You said you saw something between us, right?"

Helen smiled. "I did and I do. It is clear you both have feelings for each other."

Max blinked. He didn't think it was clear Alyssa had

feelings for him. In fact, she seemed determined to avoid contact with him. "I like Alyssa, really like her, but she knows about my past. I guess you could say I was never into relationships. Now that Peyton's here, I am starting to look at things differently, but I'm not sure Alyssa sees that. How can I get her to give me a chance?"

There was no shock on Helen's face at his words, which made him wonder if he exuded the aura of a playboy. "I don't think you will win her with words. You must show her you've changed."

"I could barely get her to agree to lunch tomorrow after Tuesday night."

"Alyssa is looking for something more. She's looking for an equal. You will have to try things she is interested in." Helen looked at him matter-of-factly. "You'll have to go to church, and not just go, but give it a real effort."

Church. The word used to send shivers through his body, but if that's what it would take to show Alyssa he was changing, then he could do it. What's the worst that could happen? Losing a few hours on Sunday morning didn't sound that bad.

He nodded. "Church. Okay, I'll give it a shot."

"Good. I'll be praying for you both."

The words should surprise him, but they didn't. Helen seemed to embody the same peace and love that Alyssa had, and Max wondered if there was something to their beliefs.

As Helen left, Peyton filled him in on the rest of her day.

"We read this book about trains, and we blew bubbles outside. She's really fun."

Max smiled at her sweet voice and made a promise to himself that whatever happened with Sarah, he would be in Peyton's life from now on.

*A*lyssa woke with butterflies in her stomach on Friday. She hadn't spoken to Max since Tuesday night, but that hadn't stopped her from thinking about him. Even though she knew he was not the kind of man she should fall for, she couldn't help thinking about the "what ifs." What if he could change? What if she could convince him to attend church with her? What if he became a believer? Though there was much about him not to like, she had seen those glimpses of the man he could be.

It was just lunch today though. She needed to put the "what ifs" aside and focus on this just being lunch. She needed to keep her head on her shoulders and listen to it rather than her heart.

After a shower, Alyssa dried off and stood in her closet, surveying the offerings. What did one wear to "just a lunch?" Were shorts too casual? Was a dress too dressy? She had no idea where they were going for lunch; she should have asked him.

Deciding a longer summer dress would fit wherever they went, she pulled one over her head and put on a little makeup. Her skin was so fair and pure that she didn't need much, but decided a little powder to highlight her eyes and a touch of gloss on her lips wouldn't be too much.

With her make up done, she headed to the kitchen to make breakfast and do her devotional. It was her favorite time of day because Roxy usually slept late and she had the table to herself. Since she had no final today, she could take her time and really get into the word.

As she sipped her tea, she opened the Bible to the book of Psalm she had been reading. Psalm 34:4 jumped out at her. "I prayed to the Lord, and he answered me. He freed me from all my fears." Perhaps she needed to spend even more time in prayer to hear the Lord's answer.

❧

When she entered Max's office building a few hours later, she was greeted by two receptionists behind a large white desk. The building was bright and open with lots of natural light coming in.

"Can I help you?"

One receptionist was on the phone, chatting through the headset covering her right ear. The other, an attractive brunette, was the one who had addressed Alyssa.

"Yes, I'm here to see Maxwell Banks. Alyssa Miller."

The woman's eyes widened as she appraised Alyssa. "Just one moment. Is he expecting you?"

Alyssa nodded as the woman clicked a button on her phone handset. "Mr. Banks, there's an Alyssa here to see you." She paused, and her eyes flicked to Alyssa again. "Yes, sir, right away." She clicked the button to hang up the call and raised her eyebrow at Alyssa. "He'll see you now. Take the elevator to the third floor. His office is 307."

"Thank you." Alyssa wondered if the woman's odd reaction was because Maxwell often had women come in and she didn't fit the model or if it was because he rarely had women come in.

As the elevator opened onto the third floor, Alyssa found herself staring into the face of a man with sandy brown hair. His green eyes locked on hers and then traveled down her body, sending a thread of disgust down Alyssa's spine.

"Well, hello, I haven't seen you here before. Who can I help you find?" His voice was rich, but it didn't erase the creepy feeling he gave Alyssa.

"I'm here to see Maxwell Banks."

Surprise alighted the man's face. "Maxwell is my best friend. I'm Justin. I'll take you to him."

He stuck out his hand, but Alyssa didn't want to touch it. However, her upbringing had always taught her it was rude not to return a shake, so she swallowed her unease and took his offered hand.

"You don't have to do that. Weren't you waiting for the elevator?"

"Oh, it's no big deal. I can catch it again in a minute."

Alyssa pasted a smile on her face and followed him through the open room that housed cubicles. A few employees looked up as they passed, but no one spoke to them.

Justin deposited her in front of office 307 but not before knocking at the door jamb and announcing her to Max.

"Your lunch date is here."

Alyssa looked to Maxwell. He must have told Justin because she sure hadn't.

"Thanks, Justin."

Justin hung just a moment longer before leaving when Maxwell said nothing more to him.

"Sorry about that," Maxwell said when they were alone. "He means well, but Justin…" He didn't finish the statement, just shrugged. "Anyway, are you ready?"

"Sure."

They garnered even more looks as they walked back through the office and to Maxwell's car.

"So, I have to ask," she said as he opened the car door for her, "do you have a lot of women visit you at work or am I the only one?"

His head tilted to the side as a lopsided smile pulled at his mouth. "Why do you ask?"

"Because I received rather strange, disbelieving looks from the moment I stepped into your building." She stretched the belt across her chest and snapped it into the clasp.

Maxwell stared at her as if deciding how much to tell her. "You are the first woman I have let come to my work," he said finally. "In the past, I never wanted to see the women again, so I didn't want them showing up at my job."

A tiny flicker of something burgeoned in Alyssa's heart. "So, I'm special then."

She meant it as a joke, but his face was serious as he answered her. "Yes, you're special." He flashed her a smile before turning the key and backing the car out of the space.

Alyssa's eyes dropped to her lap as a faint blush crawled across her face. That she was the first woman to attend his work gave her a fuzzy feeling.

The restaurant he pulled into was a small deli. They must have beat the lunch rush as there weren't many people inside. He led her to a small booth at the back. A brown fabric covered the seats, and a simple decor adorned the walls. Alyssa was a little surprised at the restaurant choice.

"The food is good," he said, catching her reaction. "Plus, you said this wasn't a date. I promise if you'll let me take you on a real date that the restaurant will be of higher caliber."

"Oh, I didn't," Alyssa started.

"Yes, you did, but it's okay." His lopsided smile displayed a dimple in his cheek. "I don't always dine at five-star restaurants, and I know a lot of good dives."

"Really?" She couldn't help teasing him. "Maxwell Banks crashes dives?"

Her teasing set the tone for lunch, and by the time it ended, her cheeks hurt from smiling so much.

"Thank you so much for joining me for lunch," Max said as he laid money on the table to cover the meal. "I'd love to see you again, and I've been thinking. Can I come to church with you this Sunday? I want to see what's so important to you and Peyton."

Alyssa blinked at him. "You want to come to church?"

"If you'll let me." He flashed that smile again, and Alyssa couldn't say no.

CHAPTER 10

*A*lyssa smoothed her flowered dress as she stood in front of Maxwell's door, waiting for him to open it. Her breath caught as the door swung open, and an audible gasp escaped.

"This will do then?" He smiled and gestured to his dark blue shirt and black slacks. "I wasn't sure. I don't know that I've been in a church as an adult other than for a wedding or a funeral."

Alyssa couldn't imagine never attending a church service, but then she and Maxwell had lived very different lives.

"It will do nicely. The blue really brings out your eyes." The intensity in his gaze caused her to drop her eyes. "Is Peyton ready?"

"Uh, mostly, I think." He opened the door, and she followed him to the kitchen.

She was expecting another repeat of last week but was surprised to see Peyton not only dressed but with her hair combed as well.

"You did well, Max."

He grinned and grabbed Peyton's hand. "Ready?"

"Let's go," she said, pumping her other hand in the air.

Alyssa laughed as they headed out to the garage and climbed into the Malibu. Though Maxwell drove, Alyssa directed him through each turn, and minutes later, they pulled into the parking lot of a single story white church.

"Huh, I thought it would be bigger."

"There are other churches that are, but this is the one Sarah and I went to. It's the perfect size for us. People know you so you don't feel lost."

The inside was larger than the outside seemed with a large sanctuary directly in front of them and a hallway that led to offices and meeting rooms to the right. A nursery and toddler area were to the left. Two women stood behind a brown desk at the front of the right hallway.

"Hi, can I check in Peyton Moore?"

The women's smiles faded at Alyssa's voice. "Is she…?"

"Sarah is in New York. We'll be praying for the best." Alyssa's tone was forceful but kind. She had known these questions would come, but that didn't make them any easier to answer over and over.

One of the women handed over a white sticker, and Alyssa led the way down the hallway. After placing the sticker on Peyton's back, she hugged her and sent her into a small classroom.

"What's the sticker for?" Max asked as they headed back toward the sanctuary.

"It's a safety thing. If she needs something, they will flash this number on a little box at the front of the sanctuary, and I know to go get her. I also have to show this tag to pick her up, so they don't send her off with a stranger."

"I guess that makes sense."

Alyssa led the way into the sanctuary, and Max sat beside her. His head slowly turned as he took in the surroundings. The sanctuary was large, but not overly decorated. A white screen hung at the back of the room to display the words to the songs, and a piano, drum set, and a few guitars sat on the slightly raised stage at the front.

"Hi, Alyssa, we're praying for you and Sarah." Though said in different variations, that seemed to be the mantra of the day as people she knew came up to her. She introduced Max to each one, and though most were courteous and pleased to meet him, she saw a few vainly trying to hide their contempt for the man. Unfortunately, even church goers were human and often struggled with the same sins.

The worship team took the stage a few minutes later, and Alyssa lost herself in the songs. Though Max didn't sing beside her, she caught him watching her a few times, and it created an odd sensation in her heart. She could see herself with him here each Sunday, if he could open up his heart to the possibility of God, but then there was Sarah. If she got better, wouldn't she want to get back together with Max? And if she didn't make it, would Alyssa feel guilty for being with him when Sarah couldn't?

Pastor Brown spoke on love as he took the stage, and Alyssa couldn't have asked for a more perfect message. She had been hoping it would be a nicer one that would allow Max to see the good side of God and not just the "rules part" that a lot of people got hung up on.

"What did you think?" she asked Max when the service ended.

"It was interesting."

It was hard to tell from his voice if he was being serious or dismissive, but the expression on his face suggested the former. Alyssa sent up another prayer for him as she led the way back down the hallway to get Peyton.

"Aunt Lyssa, look, we made bracelets." Peyton shoved her tiny arm in front of Alyssa's face to show off the shiny beads on the story bracelet.

"I remember these. I made one when I was a kid too."

"What does it mean?" Max touched the beads, as Peyton shoved the bracelet in his face.

Alyssa smiled as she remembered the lesson from years ago. "The black represents sin, showing that we all have sinned. The red represents Jesus's blood shed on the cross for us. Blue is for faith because sometimes you can't see with your eyes. The yellow represents eternal life, the kind we receive when we let Jesus into our hearts. Do you know what the white is Peyton?"

Her eyes closed, and her face scrunched as she tried to remember. "Uh, white is for no more sins."

"Close," Alyssa smiled, "it's for the forgiveness of our sins. I never can remember what the green is though."

"It's for growth in God's love," a woman with blond hair said as she approached the entrance. "Hi, I'm Kim. I'm Peyton's Sunday School teacher."

"Max," he said, sticking his hand out to take hers.

Alyssa watched the exchange and was surprised to feel a tiny pang of jealousy sprout in her heart. "Thanks, Kim, we'll see you next week." As she grabbed Peyton's hand, she noticed the tiny flicker of shock in Kim's eyes and the look of amusement in Max's.

"Was that jealousy?" he whispered as she marched them down the hall and toward the entrance.

"No," she hissed back, "I'm hungry. I thought we could get some lunch." The words were not convincing, even to her, and the chuckle that escaped from Max's perfect lips told her he wasn't buying it either.

"Can we go to McDonalds?"

Max and Alyssa both looked down at Peyton at the same time. She could see on his face that he didn't want to go there either.

"How about an upscale version of McDonalds?" he offered.

"Does it come with a toy?"

"No, but it comes with ice cream."

Peyton shrugged her small shoulders. "Okay then."

"Wow, I was hoping for a bigger reaction."

"Hey, you take what you can get when they're three," Alyssa said with a chuckle.

He smiled back at her and held her gaze a little longer than necessary, sending another tremor through her body.

When they reached the car, he opened the passenger door for her before helping Peyton into the car seat. Though he fumbled a little, it was clear he had been practicing strapping Peyton in.

Max was quiet as they drove, and Alyssa used the time to sneak furtive glances his direction. Perhaps this was the man Sarah fell in love with. She could see the possibility in his strong cheekbones and the tender side she had seen show itself today. *What am I thinking? I can't be equating love with this man.* But as hard as she tried to deny it, the feelings still crept in.

Max pulled into a casual bar-b-que restaurant. Although it had tables to sit at, it was definitely more fast food.

"Learned your lesson last time, huh?" Alyssa said, a teasing glint flashing in her eye.

"Yeah. I'll save the nicer restaurants for kid-free time, but this place has great food."

"I know. It's one of my favorites."

*A*s they drove back from lunch, Max sneaked glances at Alyssa. He had enjoyed the day. Her church had been different from what he expected, but in a good way. The pastor had spoken on God's love, which was something he hadn't heard much in the past. If that trend continued, he might find himself tolerating church.

Lunch had even gone well. There had been a few harrowing moments when Peyton nearly upturned her plate, and he'd had to apologize profusely for the mess she left on the table, but all in all, he considered it a success. Now, if he could just get Alyssa to go out with him again.

His eyes slid to her as the thought seared through his brain. She hadn't given him any new indications that she was interested other than her teasing interactions, but he had caught her looking his way a few times. Her face was turned out the window currently, watching the scenery pass by, and he wondered what was going on in her head. He hadn't been this curious about a woman since Sarah. Ah, but there was the rub. What if Sarah got better? Shouldn't he try to make it work with her since he knew about Peyton now? He had no business developing feelings for Alyssa. There was just too much muck in the middle.

She flashed him a small smile as they pulled into his garage. The desire to ask her to stay pounded in his head. They could have some alone time after Peyton went down for a nap, but fear of her answer kept his mouth shut. He was afraid she would say no, which would crush him, but even more afraid she would say yes, showing she felt something for him too. How awkward this felt. Maxwell Banks had never second guessed himself when it came to women, yet here he was waffling like a school boy.

Peyton was nearly half asleep as he unstrapped her

from the car seat. She felt like a ton of bricks as he carried her inside.

As he laid her in the bed, her eyes fluttered open. "Will you keep me?"

The question caught him off guard as he tucked Peyton into bed. "What do you mean?"

"I mean if my mom dies. Will you keep me or will you send me to foster care?"

His heart broke a little that such a tiny creature was worried about such big issues. "Peyton, I didn't think I wanted kids, but I honestly can't imagine my life without you in it now."

"Thanks, Max."

Max, it was like a slap in the face. He shouldn't expect her to call him Dad or Daddy; it had only been a week but hearing her call him Max didn't sit well either. He leaned in and kissed her forehead before exiting her room and returning to the living room.

"What's the matter?" Alyssa asked as he entered.

Max shook his head. He almost didn't want to say the statement aloud, but Alyssa's face softened his resolve, and the words began to spill out. "She called me Max. I know it's still early, but... I don't know, is it crazy that I want her to call me Dad?" His hand ran across his forehead as he said the word, a gesture he hadn't done in ages.

"No, I don't think it's crazy. Knowing you have a

child—your own flesh and bone—does crazy things to you, but," she laid her hand on his arm, "she doesn't see that yet. She needs to know that you'll take care of her and protect her before she'll feel safe enough to open up her heart."

His eyes dropped from her emerald gaze to the pale hand on his arm. Could she feel the heat that was radiating up his arm at her touch? As his eyes moved back up, they stopped on her perfect lips. Full and pink, he longed to know what they would feel like pressed against his. Her lips parted slightly as she noticed his focus. That would normally be his cue, but he wanted to be sure. He flicked his eyes back to hers and a jumble of emotions poured out of them. He could sense her desire, but also her confusion and trepidation.

Suddenly, the warmth receded from his arm. She had pulled her hand away. "Well, I guess I should be going."

"Are you leaving already?" His heart constricted at the thought.

"Do I have a reason to stay?"

Her words opened the door for him to make his move, but suddenly his throat was dry. He never lost his cool around women, so why was he finding himself tongue tied now? He took a step toward her. His hands wanted to reach out to touch her, but an invisible barrier kept them glued to his side. Still, the closeness caused her to take a breath.

"I'd like you to stay." His voice was low and throaty. He cleared his throat as he took another small step toward her. The unseen heat building between them billowed over him.

"Max, I… "

The hesitation was evident in her eyes, and it killed him.

"I know you know about my reputation, but having Peyton and meeting you… I feel different."

Her head shook slowly, but not as if she was saying no, more like as if she was trying to convince herself.

"Will you give me a chance to show you at least?" This time his hand did reach out and cup her face. She leaned into his hand, and he couldn't fight the feelings any longer. He pulled her close and touched her lips ever so slightly with his own. It was more breath and expectation than actual kiss, but it was enough to send a shock through his lips and a tremor through Alyssa's body.

Her eyes snapped open, and she pulled back. "Max, I don't know if I can do this."

"Alyssa, if you can promise to at least give me a shot, I'll do my best to show you a different Max."

Her lip pulled into her mouth as her teeth bit down

on it. It was the cutest gesture he had ever seen, but his heart thudded in his chest as he waited for her answer.

"The nanny, Helen, she sees it. There's something here, Alyssa."

"I... I will think about it, Max. I'll call you later."

As Alyssa hurried out of his house again, Max sighed and leaned his head back. He'd have to come up with some way to win her over.

*A*lyssa didn't stop moving until she was at her car, but as she fumbled for her keys, she nearly dropped them; her hands were shaking so badly. Once inside, she grasped the steering wheel to try to calm herself before driving. Why had she run again? She had wanted him to kiss her; she had liked him kissing her. Was that the problem? Was it that she liked it too much?

When her heart had slowed its rhythm down, she inserted the keys and started the engine. Though music played on the radio, she could hardly hear it, her thoughts were spinning a mile a minute. Was it possible he could have changed that quickly? He did seem different, but was it different enough?

"Lord, I need your guidance here. I know I'm developing feelings, but are they misplaced? He isn't a believer yet, but I feel like his heart was opening today.

Please guide me in your will." Saying the words out loud was like putting aloe on a burn–it soothed and calmed her nerves, and while she didn't get an immediate answer, she knew that God would answer in his own time. She just had to try to listen.

CHAPTER 11

"You missed another great party, man." Justin leaned against the door to Max's office, his arms crossed over his chest. "It was phenomenal."

"That's great, Justin, but I just don't see parties in my future right now." *Or ever again.* "I had a good weekend too. I spent the time with Peyton and Alyssa." He smiled as he remembered their first kiss. He wished it had lasted longer, but her response to it at least gave him hope that she felt something too.

"Yeah, Alyssa. She's hot, man. I can see why you dig her, but do you really want to get tied down right now? I mean you are in the prime of your life!" Justin sauntered in and plopped down in the chair across from Max's desk, stretching out his long legs and folding his arms behind his head. "There were so many beauties there on Saturday."

"There's something nice about seeing the same woman more than once though," Max replied. He shouldn't have to, but he felt the need to defend his actions. He and Justin traveled the same circles together, but now a distance was growing between them.

"I don't know about that, but I'd like to see what this woman offers that has you so intrigued. How about a double date on Friday? I'm sure I can scrounge up someone."

The proposition would have been one he jumped on a few weeks ago, but now the thought sent a feeling of dread through Maxwell. "I don't know if that's a good idea. We aren't even dating yet." *Though I'm trying.* "Just more like getting to know each other."

"That will be perfect then because I won't be dating the woman I bring either. Come on, just a dinner or a movie or something."

"I'll ask her," Max said, "but I can't promise anything."

*H*e contemplated the call to Alyssa the rest of the day but could never seem to find the right words. However, as he pulled into his driveway, he was surprised to find her car parked in front of his house.

He pulled out his phone, but there had been no missed calls. *What is she doing here?*

The sound of laughter greeted him as he entered the house, and as he placed his mug on the bar, he spied Helen, Alyssa, and Peyton in the living room. Alyssa was tickling Peyton on the floor and all three were giggling.

Peyton noticed him first and struggled to her feet. "Max." A smile of sheer delight lit up her face and she ran to him. He bent down to hug her, enjoying the sensation of her happiness to see him. "Aunt Lyssa is here. She's playing tickle monster." Peyton wiggled her fingers at Max to demonstrate.

"I see that," he said, laughing. "You guys look like you're having fun." His eyes caught Alyssa's gaze before she dropped her eyes to the floor.

"Can she stay for dinner, please?"

Max could think of nothing he would like more. "It's up to Alyssa. It's perfectly fine with me. Helen, you are welcome to stay too." Though he hoped she would say no, it would have been rude not to invite her.

"Oh no, dearie. I have my grandbabies coming over tonight. I best be getting home to them, but I put a Shepherd's pie in the oven. It ought to be enough to feed three." She winked at Max as she gathered her things.

"See you tomorrow, Peyton. Thanks for the visit, Alyssa."

"You're welcome," Alyssa said, rising from the floor.

"Well, would you like to stay for dinner?" Max asked again.

Alyssa opened her mouth, but before she could utter a word, Peyton grabbed her hand. "Please, Aunt Lyssa?"

"How do you say no to that?" she asked, laughing. "Okay, I'll stay."

"Good. Why don't you grab some plates and I'll get the pie out of the oven?" Max asked. He grabbed two pot holders and opened the oven. The smell of meat, vegetables, and potatoes wafted out. Reaching in with the potholders, he grabbed the sides of the casserole dish and pulled it out. White wisps of steam rose into the air as he carried it to the table and set it in the middle.

Alyssa had already placed three plates on the table and filled glasses—milk for Peyton and iced tea for Max and herself. She helped push Peyton in before taking her own seat. Max sat last.

"Will you join us for prayer this time?" Alyssa asked.

"Sure." Max was surprised when, instead of clasping her hands together as before, she reached out and took ahold of his hand. He smiled at her before following suit and taking Peyton's hand. It still felt odd to close his eyes, but he enjoyed the warmth of Alyssa's hand as the darkness took over.

"Lord, thank you for this food and for the many blessings that you have given us. Help us to keep our eyes on you in everything we do. Amen."

Peyton echoed the amen, and Max scooped Shepherd's Pie onto everyone's plate.

After dinner, Peyton tugged his arm, dragging him into the living room.

"Can we watch a movie, Max, please?"

Max looked to Alyssa who shrugged as if to say she had nowhere to be. She took one edge of the couch and Peyton crawled up beside her, leaving the other end free for Max. He flicked on Moana, Peyton's current favorite movie of the hour, and claimed his seat.

Though Peyton sat in between them, Max could feel Alyssa's presence just a foot away. Her perfume drifted in the air, igniting his senses. He longed to reach over and clasp her hand again, but he had no idea what Alyssa would do and there was Peyton to consider.

By the time the movie ended, Peyton was almost asleep on Alyssa's lap.

"Come on, Peyton. Let's get you into bed," Max said as he scooped her up. "Can you stay a moment?" he asked Alyssa. "There is something I want to ask you."

"Uh, sure," she answered, her voice filled with curiosity.

"Great, I'll be right back." He carried Peyton to her bedroom, changing her quickly into pajamas and laying her in bed. As she was almost asleep, he decided to skip the story and the prayer, but placed a kiss on her head and smoothed her hair back before leaving the room.

Alyssa was still on the couch when he returned though she rose as he entered.

"So, what's up?"

"My friend Justin, the one you met at the office, he wants to get together, kind of like a double date this Friday."

Alyssa sucked in her breath and looked away. "I don't know if that's a good idea."

"I know he's not your cup of tea, but he's been my friend for years, and he's trying. He said he wants to get to know you better. Just one night, please?" Max took a step toward her as he finished the plea.

"I..." Alyssa bit her bottom lip as she thought. "Okay, one night, but if it's awful, we never do it again, agreed?"

"Agreed," Max said with a laugh.

Alyssa smiled, and silence descended. Her eyes stared into Max's and, heart racing, he took another step toward her. When she didn't move, he took that as a sign and cupped her face. Her chest moved ever so slightly with her breath and he leaned down, placing his lips on hers.

Her arms wrapped around his neck, and the kiss

deepened, but as he pulled her closer, she pushed him away, breaking the contact.

"I have to go. Thank you for a wonderful night, and I'll see you Friday."

As she dashed away again, Max wondered if she would ever stop running from their attraction.

CHAPTER 12

*M*ax grabbed the flowers from his passenger seat after parking the car at Alyssa's apartment. Even though Alyssa had agreed to this date, he wondered if this double date idea was a good one.

He had found himself drifting further away from Justin, and he worried that Justin would remind Alyssa of his past. Max had been working hard to show Alyssa how much he had changed, but it was too late to change his mind now and cancel the date.

After a quick knock on the door, it swung open, but it was not Alyssa's face on the other side. A pretty blond with a nose ring greeted him.

"You must be Max. I'm Roxy, Alyssa's roommate."

Max shook the proffered hand as he wondered why

Alyssa had never mentioned a roommate. "Nice to meet you, Roxy."

Her eyes traveled up and down his body, and she raised an eyebrow at him. The very gesture made Max feel more like an item being appraised than like a man, and he vowed never again to perform it on a woman.

"Thank you, Roxy," Alyssa said as she appeared behind the blond. She was dressed in a dark green top and slacks which brought out the natural green in her eyes and made her skin appear paler than it was. The effect was almost mystical.

"You look beautiful." The words slipped out before Max could reel them back in, and Alyssa blushed.

"Thanks, you look good too."

"Ah, aren't you guys cute?"

Roxy's obnoxious intrusion broke the spell of their locked gazes, and Max pasted a smile on his face to hide his annoyance. "Here, these are for you." He handed Alyssa the bouquet of red and white carnations he had picked up on his way.

"Thank you," she said, accepting them. "Roxy, will you put these in some water for me?" She handed the flowers off and pulled the door shut behind her. "I'm sorry about her. She's a little abrasive sometimes."

"Don't worry, Justin is the same way."

"Yeah, I remember meeting him. I have to say, I'm a little nervous about a double date with him."

Max stopped and took her hands. "Can I be honest? I am too. Justin has been my friend for years, but he represents a lot of the old Max. I've felt us separating as I've tried to put that guy behind me, but it would be rude to stand them up."

"I guess you're right," Alyssa said, shrugging. "Besides, what is the worst that could happen?"

*A*n hour later, Alyssa found herself wishing she had never made that statement. Max had been trying his best to keep Justin in check, but he kept trying to bring up escapades from their past. Even worse, he didn't appear to be interested in the woman beside him as his eyes followed every woman who walked past them.

"Hey remember that time when—"

"You know, I think we'll skip dessert," Max said, interrupting him. "In fact, Alyssa has a final tomorrow, so I should get her home." He removed his wallet and placed a hundred-dollar bill on the table. "That should cover our part of the bill. You ready?"

Alyssa smiled at him. Though she didn't approve of the lie, she was immensely relieved to be leaving Justin's company.

"It was nice to meet you," she said to Justin's date, "and nice to see you again." The last five words she had to force out as she'd rather watch paint dry than go out with Justin again.

Max grabbed her hand as they exited the restaurant, and she squeezed it. She might still have some concerns about his past, but his present was showing definite promise.

"I really do want dessert," he said as they stepped into the warm summer air. "Care to accompany me to a local bakery?"

"Of course," she said, adopting his formal vocabulary. "I would be delighted."

He placed her hand on the crook of his arm and escorted her up the sidewalk and over a few blocks to a small pastry shop housed in between a clothing store and a used book shop. The Sweeter Side was stenciled in white on the glass door, and a small pink awning hung above the doorway. As he opened the door, a small bell jingled, announcing their arrival.

Delicate glass tables with white chairs dotted the inside of the shop, which was painted a pastel pink. A glass showcase spanned the wall just in front of them, ending at the cash register.

"How did you ever find this place?" Somehow, she couldn't picture the old Maxwell Banks ever stepping foot in this pretty shop.

"Actually, I know the owner."

Images of a woman from Maxwell's past flooded

Alyssa's mind, but she was not prepared for the plump, mousy brunette that appeared behind the counter. The woman was pretty, but not the type of woman she could ever see Maxwell with.

"Maxwell Banks? Is that you?" The woman's eyes lit up and she pushed her thick glasses up her nose.

"Hey, Marcy. I heard from a friend that you had opened a place here and figured it was time I tried it."

"Well, I'll be darned. I never thought I'd see the likes of you in my little 'ol shop. Maxwell and I went to high school together," she said to Alyssa, "though I don't think he knew I was alive."

"Oh, I knew," Maxwell said. "At least I did the day you baked us those brownies after our Homecoming win."

"That's right. I almost forgot about that. I suppose I should have warned the team about the nuts. Was your friend, what was his name, Doug? Was he alright?"

Max laughed and nodded his head. "He spent the night scratching a rash, but he was fine."

Alyssa smiled at this playful side of Max. Had he been more easy going in high school? If so, what had happened to him to make him change?

"Well, what can I do for you tonight?" Marcy placed her hands akimbo on her hips, reminding Alyssa of a Mrs. Butterworth's syrup bottle.

"We had to leave dinner without dessert, so we need something sweet." Max tossed a wink at Alyssa.

Marcy pursed her lips a moment and then held up a pudgy finger. "I have just the thing. Do you two like chocolate?"

Max raised his eyebrow at Alyssa, who smiled in return. "I love chocolate."

"Perfect. You two pick a table and I'll bring you something special."

As Marcy scurried out of the room, Maxwell gestured to an empty table. Marcy returned moments later with two small white plates. A petite fudgy brownie sat on each, drizzled with a white sauce and a raspberry on top.

"This is gorgeous," Alyssa said. Though it had no smell, her mouth began watering at the gooeyness she could see oozing from the chocolate.

"Thank you," Marcy said, executing a small curtsy. "This is my triple chocolate ooey gooey brownie. It may spike your blood sugar, but my customers love it. I'll leave you to try it."

She disappeared back into the kitchen area, leaving Max and Alyssa alone.

"Well, shall we?" Alyssa picked up her dainty silver fork and raised it almost like a toast.

Max smiled as he clinked her fork. "I thought you'd never ask."

As the first bite touched Alyssa's tongue, her eyes rolled back. "Oh my goodness. This is delicious." When she refocused, she realized Max wasn't eating, but watching her, and her face flamed. "Sorry, it's just so good." She dropped her eyes in embarrassment, but Max only laughed.

"Don't be sorry. You are gorgeous when you eat. I could watch you all day."

Though the conversation stalled after that, it was a comfortable silence. Alyssa enjoyed the way Max made her feel—she couldn't remember the last time a man did that—but she wondered if Max was being genuine or if this was all part of his act.

When their plates were clean, Max paid the bill and led her back outside. His hand found hers as they walked back to the car, and she didn't pull away. There was something comforting in his touch.

As they pulled into her apartment complex, she found herself wishing she lived alone so she could invite him in. It wasn't that she couldn't invite him in with Roxy there, but she never knew what Roxy would do, and it didn't invite the atmosphere she was hoping for.

He opened her door after parking the car and offered a hand to help her up, but he didn't move away once she stood. Instead he laced his fingers through her other hand so that both hands were intertwined.

"Alyssa, I really enjoyed spending time with you. I'd like to see you again."

His eyes were hypnotizing as she stared into them. She found the last pieces of her resolve that they shouldn't be together melting away. "I'd like that too."

The corners of his lips curled into a smile as he leaned down. When his lips touched hers, she didn't pull away but enjoyed the warmth of them against her own. It wasn't a long kiss, but it was enough to curl her toes and leave her breathless when he pulled away.

"Will you come tomorrow and hang out with Peyton and me? I was thinking of taking her to the park."

Alyssa nodded, her voice lost in the emotions running rampant through her body. Max smiled and took a step back. He dropped one of her hands, so they could walk side by side to the door. Once there, he gave it another squeeze and planted another soft kiss on her mouth before dropping her hand and walking away.

She stood rooted to the spot as she watched him go, wondering just what she had gotten herself into.

CHAPTER 13

Max whistled as he entered the house after dropping Alyssa off. The evening hadn't started off well, but it had certainly ended much nicer. His lips were still tingling from the kiss with Alyssa, and though he knew he hadn't won her over completely yet, it felt like he was certainly making headway.

The sound of crying broke his daydream and he quickened his pace as he headed into the living room. Peyton was curled up on Helen's lap, her face buried in the older woman's shoulder. Her small frame rose and fell with her sobs.

"It's alright, dearie. It will all be okay."

Max rushed to Peyton. "What's the matter?"

"We were watching a movie, and she said it reminded her of her mum."

"I miss my mommy."

"Oh, Peyton. We all do," he said, reaching out to stroke her back. "I'll take her," he whispered to Helen. "You can take off."

"Are you sure? I don't mind staying and helping."

Max smiled at her. "No, I'm sure. I've got this. I won't always have you or Alyssa around, so I need to figure out ways to help her myself."

Helen's lips pulled into a smile and she took Max's hand. "You will be a good daddy, no matter what. I can see it in your eyes. Here, Peyton, go to Max."

Max reached down and grasped Peyton's arms with one arm while he slid the other under her knees. With an effortless curl, he removed her from Helen's chest and flipped her over onto his.

"Don't ever leave me, Daddy."

The word cut like a knife through his heart. He loved that she called him Daddy but hated that it was due to the tragedy she was feeling in missing Sarah.

"You see? She feels it too." Helen stood and patted Max's shoulder. "Call me if you need anything. I'll see you Monday, Peyton."

Max mouthed "thank you" to her as she left the room. Then he took the place Helen had just vacated on the couch.

Though he had no magic words to make everything

better, he continued to pat Peyton's back and murmur, "It's alright."

When her body stilled, he looked down to see her asleep against his chest. Her little hand was curled into a fist near her chin and wet trails glistened on her cheeks. *How much harder will this be if Sarah doesn't get better?*

***

"She called me Daddy last night," Max said to Alyssa the next day as they sat on the bench watching Peyton play.

"Max, that's wonderful."

He sighed. "It is, but I think it's because she misses Sarah so much. She was in tears when I got home last night, and she cried herself to sleep."

"Oh, no. I'll call the treatment center and see if she's feels up to a phone call. That would help, wouldn't it?"

"Honestly, I have no idea what would help. I'm sort of going along by trial and error here."

Alyssa placed her hand on his knee. "I think you are doing a good job, especially for just a few weeks."

He glanced down at her hand before returning his gaze to Peyton, who was climbing the small ladder and sliding down the accompanying slide. "I'm just worried about what will happen if Sarah doesn't make it, you know?"

"That you have to give to God. It's in his hands now. There is nothing we can do on this end, except pray and be there for Peyton."

"Where does your faith in God come from?" he asked. "I mean, what started it all?"

Alyssa leaned back in the bench and tilted her face to the sky. "I grew up hearing all about him. My mom and my Aunt Sandra both became strong Christians before I was born, so God was always a part of my life. I didn't really develop a relationship with him though until my mom got sick. I was only a teenager the first time, and it rocked my world.

"I couldn't understand why God would let my mom get sick because she had changed her life around and become a crusader for him. My dad withdrew. I don't think he had a relationship with Jesus like my mom did, so the only one I could really talk to was Jesus and my Aunt Sandra. She taught me how to really pray and how to listen for God's voice.

"When my mom passed away a few years ago, I blamed God, but my aunt showed me all the extra time he gave me with my mom because she went into remission twice. Slowly, I started to see that God has a plan that we can't always see, and that sometimes, he answers our prayers in ways we don't expect.

"When I look back at my life, I can see that he's always been there for me." She turned her face back to

Maxwell. "I know you don't believe in him, but he's there for you too. He's just waiting for you to invite him in."

"I don't think your God would want me. You know a little of my past, but there's more." He adjusted his position to find Peyton, who had moved on from the slide and was now playing in the small house.

"That's what my Aunt Sandra thought after she got pregnant and had an abortion, but when she finally gave her life to God, he used her to save other women and their babies. God doesn't want you to wait until you're perfect because we never will be. Instead, he wants to meet you where you are and help you along the way."

"I'll think about it, and I'll keep taking Peyton to church. In fact, can we come with you again tomorrow?"

"Of course."

Alyssa's words continued to parade through Max's head as they watched Peyton play. He had never thought he needed God in his life, but he felt the need for some guidance, and if something happened to Sarah, he would definitely need some strength. He also never thought he'd like kids, but so far that had been a good change, and maybe letting God in his life would be the same.

CHAPTER 14

"You look beautiful," Max said to Alyssa as he opened the door. In his hand was a bouquet of wild flowers, which he handed to her.

After their park date and church the next day, Max convinced Alyssa to join them for dinner. It hadn't been a hard sell as she enjoyed spending time with him though she still worried she was developing feelings for a man she shouldn't be.

"Come on in. We'll put them in some water for now and you can talk to Peyton."

As she followed him into the kitchen area, she couldn't help but notice his appearance. Though it wasn't what she was looking for long term, it always managed to grab her attention when she first saw him.

His shoulders filled out his dark blue shirt and tapered into a narrow waist. His black slacks sat nicely on his lower half. She averted her eyes as the warmth started to spread across her face.

"Aunt Lyssa."

Peyton's voice grabbed her attention, and Alyssa leaned down to hug her. "Hey, Peyton, how are you doing?"

"Good, do you like your flowers? I helped Daddy pick them."

"They are beautiful, thank you."

"Hello, Alyssa. Nice to see you again."

Alyssa looked up to see Helen. "Hello, Helen. It's nice to see you too." Her voice held just a hint of curiosity as she thought the dinner was going to be the three of them.

"Helen's going to watch Peyton, so we can enjoy a nice dinner without distractions." Max smiled at her as he took the flowers and placed them in a crystal vase he pulled down from a cabinet while she was talking to Peyton.

"Oh, well, that's wonderful." Inside her heart had started a steady increase at the thought. Alone with Max at a nice restaurant? She could see two outcomes to this—firecrackers or disaster.

"Don't hurry home," Helen said, smiling at them. "I can hold the fort down here."

"Why do I feel like she knows something I don't know?" Alyssa asked in a lowered voice as she and Max headed back outside.

Max laughed. "Right? I always feel like that around Helen too."

The smile that lit up his handsome face caused a flutter in Alyssa's heart. He reached for her hand as they stepped outside the house and she squeezed his back. Though she still wasn't sure how she felt about his past, she couldn't deny that he appeared to be changing in front of her. Besides, the feeling of warmth that crept up her arms at his touch was too nice to let go of for now.

Opening the door, he helped her into the seat. Only then did he let go of her hand, and immediately she missed the warmth.

"Where are we going?" she asked as he slid into the driver's seat. They were in his BMW, and she could see why he didn't want to get rid of the car. The leather on the seats molded itself to her body, and she felt like she was sitting on foam.

"Do you like Italian?" He glanced at her with a sly smile.

Did she like Italian? Her mother, while not Italian, used to cook her own pasta at home, so Alyssa grew up eating Italian. In fact, one of the things she missed the most was her mother's cooking.

"Love it," she answered and couldn't tame the smile spreading across her own lips.

When they arrived at the restaurant, he hurried to open her door and took her hand once again. This time his fingers laced through hers and fit like a glove.

The inside of the restaurant was dark, lit only by dim overhead lights and candles at each table. A woman in a black dress with a white belt greeted them from behind a podium.

"Welcome to Il Piacere. Do you have a reservation?" Her voice was laced with just the slightest Italian accent.

"Yes, it's under Maxwell Banks."

Her eyes scanned a list in front of her. "Ah, yes, here you are Mr. Banks. Right this way."

She led the way to a back-corner table just big enough for two. A white table cloth draped the table top and white china plates sat at each side. Bright silverware lay on black cloth napkins that lined the right side of the plate. Two crystal glasses resided in front of each plate.

"Would you like some wine? Our house specialty is a red merlot tonight."

"Yes, that would be lovely, thank you." Max nodded at the hostess and then held the chair out for Alyssa to sit before taking his own seat. "I hope that was okay. I forgot to ask if you drink wine."

"I don't drink much, but as this is a special occasion, I'll partake."

"I hope it will be the first of many special occasions." He reached across the table and grabbed her hand as he smiled at her.

"Well, I was talking about passing my finals," she said with a shy smile, "but this is pretty good too."

"You passed your finals? That's fantastic, Alyssa." He squeezed her hand, sending another shot of warmth up her arm.

The waitress appeared then with a bottle of wine and a plate of bread. The plate she placed in between them, smiling at their joined hands. The wine she poured into Max's glass. "Try a taste, sir? Make sure it is to your liking?"

Max lifted the glass with his right hand, swirled it around, sniffed it, and finally took a sip. He had obviously done this before. "It is wonderful, thank you."

The waitress nodded and then filled his glass and Alyssa's. "Here is the menu for you." She handed over a single white sheet with about nine items on it. "Our special tonight is four-cheese tortellini. I'll give you a minute to look over the menu."

With a quick nod, she turned and walked away. Her brown hair was pulled into a loose bun and a few tendrils curled at the nape of her neck.

Alyssa scanned the offerings, her eyes widening at the prices. Though she assumed this was a date, she would hate to presume he was paying only to find out she must cover a fifty-dollar meal.

"Order what you want. Don't worry about the prices." His voice was soft and non-judgmental.

"Am I that obvious?" A faint heat stole across her cheeks.

"No, but when you have money like I do, sometimes you forget not everyone does. Tonight is on me, and I want you to choose what you want."

She nodded and returned her focus to the menu. There were two types of salad, four entrees, and three desserts listed. Though they all looked good, she decided on the special. After all, it was probably the special for a reason.

After the order was placed, Max squeezed her hand. "Tell me a little more about you."

"Hmm, well, I'm an only child. My parents always wanted more but couldn't get pregnant after me. I left Mesquite, where I'm from, when I was eighteen to go to school here. What else do you want to know?"

"How did you and Sarah meet?"

Alyssa smiled as she remembered the meeting. "At church, actually. She came in wanting help with an unplanned pregnancy. Said she thought the father would push her to have an abortion, so she left without telling him, but she had no family and needed some help. Would you have?"

Max blinked at her, clearly taken off guard. "Would I have what?"

"Would you have pushed her to have an abortion?"

After taking a deep breath, Max leaned back and ran a hand through his hair. "I'd like to say no. I mean Sarah meant more to me than anyone I had dated. I hope I would have said I'd stay with her, but I can't know for sure. As you know, I was not ready to settle down then, and I hate to think I might have pushed her to get rid of Peyton, but..."

He couldn't finish the sentence, and Alyssa was almost sorry she asked. "Do you think you're ready to settle down now?"

His hand rubbed across his chin as he considered her. "I didn't think I'd ever be ready to settle down, but then Peyton came into my life and I met you. I think I could be ready to settle down with the right person."

"Hah, don't listen to him honey."

Surprised, Alyssa glanced up to see a chesty blond in a tight shirt standing at the end of their table.

"That's nearly the same line he used on me before he 'lost my number.'" The woman made air quotes as she said the last three words before placing her hands on her hips. "How ya doing, Max?"

The color drained from Max's face as he looked from the blond to Alyssa. "I'm doing all right, and I'm sorry I didn't call."

"No, you're not. You're just sorry I ran into you and am ruining your date, along with your chance to score tonight. I bet you can't even remember my name, can you?"

Max opened his mouth as if he was going to say her name, but then he closed it and shook his head. His eyes dropped to the table momentarily before flicking back up to the woman. "No, I can't, and I'm sorry."

The woman turned to Alyssa. "Get out now while you can honey." Then she turned her furious eyes on Max and spat out two words, "It's Iris," before stomping away and leaving a stunned Alyssa staring at Max.

"You didn't even remember their names?" Her voice was barely more than a whisper.

Max hung his head. "To be honest, I didn't even know their names to begin with most of the time."

"How many have there been?"

Max's eyes slid to the side, avoiding the questions. "More than I'd like to tell you, but there wasn't a woman every weekend. It was just a different woman every time."

Alyssa sucked in her breath, disgusted and shocked. All the walls that had been crumbling the past week began rebuilding rapidly.

"But I'm not like that anymore," Max hurried on. He reached for her hand, but Alyssa pulled it back and folded it in her lap. "I don't want that life anymore. Peyton changed me. You changed me."

"Stop," she said, holding up her hand. Though her heart wanted to believe him, every other sensible part of her body was screaming at her to run, that he would be just like the guy in college. "I don't know what to think right now, and I need a little time to process."

Her heart ached when she saw Max's face fall, but she must protect herself. The food arrived a few minutes after, but the mood was broken. They finished their food in silence and opted for no dessert. This was not the night she had been hoping for. Would going out with Max be like this all the time? Even if he had changed, would the endless parade of his past never cease?

*M*ax stared at Alyssa across the table and let out a small sigh. This was not the night he had been hoping for. He had wanted to show her the new Max, but Iris showing up had just reminded her of his past, and he couldn't blame her.

The look on Iris's face had been one of anger but also guilt. He had never thought about how the women must feel the next day when he didn't call them back or return their calls, but as he looked at Alyssa's face, he could see a sadness there that he imagined the other women must have felt, especially because he hadn't been honest about his intentions.

The rest of the meal passed in silence, torturing him. He wanted to try to explain himself, but she had made it clear that she needed space, and if he was going to prove he'd changed, then he would have to honor her wishes.

He didn't try to hold her hand as they walked back to the car, but he did still open the door for her. She flashed him a tight smile, but even that small gesture encouraged him. He might have to work harder, but the fact that she was looking at him at all, was a start.

The ride back to his house was also mute, but as he pulled into the driveway, he tried one more time. "Alyssa, I'm really sorry. This isn't how I wanted the night to go. I know I have a past, but I am trying to change."

"I believe you are." Her voice was quiet, but at least she was looking at him. "I just need some time to think things over. Will you tell Peyton good night for me?"

"Wait, don't you want to take your flowers?"

A look of indecision crossed her face, but after a sigh, she agreed and followed him into the house.

"Aunt Lyssa. You're back."

"We sure are, sweetie. Did you have fun with Helen?"

It floored Max how she could turn on her happy voice that quickly when she had been reserved with him for the last hour.

"Uh huh." Peyton nodded her head up and down enthusiastically.

"We made dinner and then we colored," Helen said, rising from the table. She looked from Alyssa to Max but said nothing though Max could see the questions in her eyes.

"That's great. Well, I have an early day tomorrow, so I'm going to get my flowers and call it a night. I'll see you soon, Peyton." With a quick nod at Max, Alyssa turned and walked out of the kitchen.

"Peyton, why don't you go play with your doll for a minute while I chat with Max?" Though it was meant as a question, it came out more like a statement from Helen's mouth, and Peyton agreed without arguing. "I take it the night didn't go as planned."

Max sighed and ran his hand across his forehead. "No, it started off well, but then a woman from my past showed up and told Alyssa not to trust me. It was awful, Helen. I finally felt like I was making progress, but now I feel like I'm back at square one."

Helen motioned for him to sit at the bar and then crossed to the stove and set the kettle to boiling. As if she owned the place, she rummaged around in the pantry for tea and pulled out two mugs. Max watched her, waiting for words of wisdom, but she said nothing as she waited for the kettle to boil. When it started to whistle, she flicked the knob to off and poured steaming water into both mugs before joining him at the bar.

"Back in England, we believe that tea can help your mind think more clearly. Drink up." She lifted her own mug to her lips and Max followed suit though he wasn't usually a tea drinker. "Your past is not something you can change, but you can change your future."

"What's the point of changing my future if my past is always going to rear its ugly head?" Max took another sip of the warm liquid, surprised to find that he liked it.

"Perhaps it is because you are trying to change superficially?"

"What do you mean?"

"I mean you are trying to change your actions, but you're trying to do it all alone. We are all imperfect creatures, and as hard as we try, we will all make mistakes, but those of us who have Jesus in our lives get the extra help of the Holy Spirit inside us. He helps us make better decisions and people can often see a physical change from having him inside."

"I've been going to church, but I'm not sure I'm ready to make a decision like that."

Helen smiled as she sipped her tea. "Then are you sure you're ready to seriously date a woman who is?"

Her words rattled around in his head as he pondered them. Was his lack of faith keeping them apart? Would that be enough to convince her he had really changed?

"What's up with you?" Roxy asked as Alyssa entered the door of their shared apartment.

"It's Max. We had dinner tonight, and it was going great, but then one of his one-night stands recognized him and came over. She told me not to trust him, and now I don't know what to think." Alyssa collapsed on the couch, dropping her head into her hands.

Roxy shut the book she was reading to give her full attention to Alyssa. "I know I met him, but all I saw was his hotness. How old is he?"

"I don't know. Late twenties, I guess." Alyssa's voice was muffled by her hands.

"I know you don't want to hear this, but not everyone grew up in faith like you. For those of us who didn't, sleeping with people isn't unheard of. In fact, most of us do it a lot."

"I know that, but he is—or was—I don't know, a serial one-night stander. What if he just wants one night with me? What if he's like Tyson?"

"Who's Tyson?"

Alyssa dropped her hands and looked up at Roxy. "You know Tyson, the guy from my Freshman year who only wanted to sleep with me and dumped me when I wouldn't?"

"Ah." Roxy nodded, her blond hair skimming her shoulders with the motion. Roxy wasn't around when Tyson happened, but Alyssa had filled her in during one of their late-night conversations about why she was waiting for marriage to be intimate. "Well, you said Max was trying to change, right?"

Alyssa nodded as she grabbed the pillow next to her and hugged it to her chest.

"Okay, then you have to understand he can't change his past. It's always going to be there. You have to decide if you are okay with it or not."

Though the words made perfect sense in her head, that was the problem. She wasn't sure if she could find a way to be okay with it or not.

$\mathcal{M}$ ax picked up his phone and punched the button again. The welcome screen flashed the time, but no new messages. He hadn't heard from Alyssa since she left Tuesday night, and it was now Friday. He wanted to give her time, but now he wondered if he should call her and try pleading his case again.

"Hey man," Justin said poking his head in the door.

Max dropped the phone, sending it clattering across the desk.

"Still no word, huh?"

"No, do you think I should call her?"

"I think," Justin said, crossing the floor to sit in the chair opposite Max's desk, "that you should come out with me tonight. Everyone is going to be there, and it will get your mind off this woman for a bit. Maybe it will clear your thinking, and you'll know what you want to do tomorrow."

"I don't know." Max's words came out in a large sigh. "I don't feel like partying much anymore and you remember what happened last time."

"You don't have to party. Just come and have a few drinks with us." Justin leaned in, placing his hands on the desk. "Everyone has been asking about you man, and it's my birthday. Just come say 'hi,' at least."

Max pressed the button on the phone one more time even though he knew she hadn't called or texted as he would have heard it. The screen was indeed blank of any contact. Just the time of 5:55 on his screen. "Okay," he sighed, "let me call Helen and ask if she can stay a little later with Peyton."

Justin smiled and pumped his fist near his chest. "Awesome, it will be great to have you back. Billionaire Banks rides again."

Max wasn't back as he was only going because it was Justin's birthday. He picked up his phone and called Helen, who agreed to watch Peyton until he returned home. She didn't comment on his decision to go out, but he could hear the admonishing tone in her voice.

"All right, let's go," he said when the clock struck six. Knowing Justin, he had this party set at one of the hotspots that had a happy hour. Hopefully, Max could get in, grab a few drinks, and then find a nice way to excuse himself so he could go home and indulge in his misery. He snickered at the thought as he realized he was becoming like the women he so desperately avoided.

They decided to take two cars, so Max could leave when he wanted. Plus, Justin would probably be taking a woman home, and Max had no plan to do so.

Sure enough, they pulled into Club Z, a popular hangout for the after-work crowd in their late twenties and thirties. Max sighed as he exited the car. Club Z was always full of beautiful women looking to meet up with the newest guy, and for some reason, they seemed to be able to smell his wealth.

The bouncer was a broad man about their age with bulging biceps and brick shoulders, and he waved them through without bothering to check their IDs. He knew them both by sight; that was how often they came here.

Inside, the club was dimly lit. Couches and tables filled one end of the room for those not dancing who wanted to try to hold a conversation. An expansive dance floor took up the middle space. The DJ booth sat in the middle above it, blasting out the latest hip hop songs. Though it was early, the crowd on the dance floor was already large and the bodies were jockeying for positions. To the left was the bar. Three bartenders in white shirts manned the bar, grabbing glasses from a silver rack above it and filling them with liquid to hand either to the waitress or the patrons.

"Let's get a couch," Max yelled and pointed to the right. Justin nodded, and the two secured a large brown couch as far away from the music as possible. "Great place for conversations." The sarcasm was evident in Max's voice. Though the music was quieter here, he still was forced to raise his voice to be heard.

"We aren't here to converse." Justin flashed him an eyebrow raise and motioned the waitress over.

"Right." Max looked down at his watch, wishing he had just said 'no' and gone home to Peyton. She'd be eating dinner right now and filling him in on her day. Maybe she would have even heard from Alyssa, who still seemed to be stopping in to see Peyton even though she was avoiding Max, and could give him some Intel. He should have just swallowed his pride and called Alyssa to try to smooth things over again.

"Max, how are you buddy? Heard you got shackled with a kid." Chris Moore, another friend of Justin's, slid onto the couch next to him.

"I wouldn't call it shackled. Peyton is great. I'm glad I'm getting the chance to know her." Max tried to keep his voice light, but inside he was seething. Was this what he sounded like a few weeks ago? The thought created a wad of disgust in his throat.

"What'll you have?" The waitress, a blond woman in

tight black shorts and a tighter white shirt, stood looking at him.

"Just a coke, thanks," Max said, but Justin jumped in before the woman could leave.

"Uh-uh, man, you promised to have at least one drink."

"Fine, a rum and coke then, but just one."

The waitress raised her eyebrow as if she had heard that line before and traipsed back to the bar.

Before she returned with their drinks, three women joined them at the couch. It was clear from their glassy eyes that they had been drinking and were well on their way to being drunk.

"My name is Amber," the brunette who had decided to leach onto Max said. She was pretty with dark hair and brown eyes, though she wore more makeup than he generally preferred, but she didn't hold a candle to Alyssa.

"Max," he said and scooted just a bit away from her. She didn't take the hint though and curled up even closer to him.

"I like Max, like Mad Max, you know that old show? You kind of even look like Mel Gibson." She placed her hand on his arm and batted her eyes.

He did look a little like Mel Gibson, albeit it a younger version, but the flattery did nothing for him this time. The waitress returned with their drinks before he could respond, and Max tossed back a swig of the drink.

"Ooh, can I have a strawberry daiquiri?" the woman beside him asked. Her friends quickly chimed in with their orders as well.

The waitress raised her brow and glanced at the men. The silent question of who was claiming responsibility for these drunk girls was evident in her stare.

"Don't worry," Justin said, "We'll make sure they get home okay."

Max wanted to kick him. He didn't want to have to worry about getting these women home; he hadn't planned on staying that long.

After another long look, the waitress shrugged and walked off to fill the girls' order.

"So, what do you do?" The woman was competing for his attention again.

"I work in advertising." Another swig and his drink was half gone. He might have to order another just to get through another hour in this place. Chris and his woman had meandered to the dance floor though Max wasn't sure you could classify what they were doing as dancing.

"Do you want to dance?" Amber asked, following his gaze.

"No, I don't dance."

The waitress returned with frothy, fruity drinks for the women and Max was granted a few minutes of blissful relief as Amber sucked her straw.

"Another?" the waitress asked, nodding her head at his nearly empty drink.

Max glanced down at the drink, then at the woman next to him. "One more," he said, though he promised himself he wouldn't.

By the time his second drink arrived, Amber had finished her first and was back to rambling on, this time about her exercise routine. Her lithe physique hadn't gone unnoticed—though he had tried his best to avoid his gaze lingering there—but he didn't need her regimen detailed either.

"I'm going to hit the bathroom. I'll be back in a minute." He hated having to announce his intentions to the woman, but it would be rude to just get up and walk away.

The bathroom was over by the bar, so he was forced to traverse the crowd on the dance floor to get there. At least twice, female hands reached out to him to entice him to dance, and he had to untangle himself from their grips.

Finally, he reached his destination and pushed open the men's room door. A few minutes later, he was navigating the gauntlet again to return to the table.

Only Amber sat there now, nursing another drink. "Where is Justin and your friend?"

She giggled and shrugged. "I think they left, if you get my meaning."

Max sighed. Just what he needed. "Okay, well how about your other friend?"

Another shrug. "Haven't seen her either."

Annoyance flared through him as his eyes rolled. "Right, well I can't leave you here alone, and I'm leaving, so I guess you're coming with me."

"I thought you'd never ask." She fell against his chest as she tried to stand.

Max wrapped an arm around her to steady her and led her to the bar to settle his tab. The bartender flashed him an eyebrow wiggle and a knowing smile which Max ignored as he signed the receipt.

Amber was nearly passed out as he got her to the door. The outside air woke her just enough to allow her to stumble to the car. Max had to hold her up more than once as they crossed the parking lot. She was in no shape to tell him where she lived.

He folded her into the passenger seat where she curled up and closed her eyes. Great, what now? He whipped out his phone to call Justin, hoping her friend had drank less and could give him directions, but the call went to voicemail.

"Justin? It's Max. You left me with Amber, and she's

passed out. I have no idea where she lives. Call me as soon as you get this, so I can take her home." He could barely hide the agitation in his voice as he punched the end call button. His only option now was to take her back to his place and hope Justin called soon.

As Amber was still passed out in the car when he pulled into the garage, Max left her there for a moment while he checked to see if Peyton was asleep. Though the situation was innocent, he didn't want her seeing a woman coming into the house.

"That was an early night," Helen said, smiling at him as he entered the kitchen.

"Yeah, unfortunately it isn't over yet. Is Peyton asleep?" He glanced around for her as the words left his mouth.

"Yes, I put her down a few minutes ago. Why?" There was an edge in Helen's voice that was more than idle curiosity.

"Justin left me with a drunk girl. I couldn't leave her there when her friends left, so I was going to take her home. Unfortunately, she drank so much she passed out, and I have no idea where she lives. I was going to let her sleep it off in the other guest room and take her home when Justin calls me back or she wakes up, which ever happens sooner, but I didn't want Peyton seeing her come in."

"Are you sure that's a good idea?" Helen asked.

"No, but I don't have many other options."

"I could take her to my house," Helen offered.

"Thank you, Helen, but she doesn't know you, and I don't want to scare the girl too much."

Helen tipped her head. "All right, if you're sure." The raise of her eyebrow let Max know she didn't like this plan, but he didn't either. However, he had little choice.

"I am. Thanks, Helen, and I'll see you Monday."

After Helen gathered her purse and bid him goodnight, Maxwell headed back to the car. Amber was still passed out in the passenger seat, her mouth open and a tiny line of drool tracking down the right side of her mouth.

Max unfastened her seat belt and snaked an arm behind her back. Her other arm he draped over his shoulder, holding her right hand in his. She was dead weight, but he managed to extricate her from the car this way. Then he dropped her right arm and squatted to slip his arm under her knees and pick her up. He was glad she didn't weigh much and that he worked out, but dead weight was still heavy.

Thankfully, the door to the house hadn't closed completely behind him, and he was able to push it open with his shoulder and shuffle down the hall to the other guest bedroom. That door was closed, and he was forced to drop her legs to open it. She let out a muffled grunt, but her eyes remained closed. How much had she had to drink?

After the door was open, he scooped her back up and crossed to the bed. He laid her down gently, pulling the covers out from under her and then back over her body. She looked young as her brown hair splayed across the white pillow, and he wondered how old she really was.

Shaking his head, he exited the room and headed down the hallway. A quick check on Peyton revealed her asleep in her bed, so he continued to his own room.

As he pulled his phone out of his pocket, he checked the screen, but there had been no call from Justin or Alyssa. Sighing, he plugged it into the charger and changed for bed. As his head hit the pillow, he decided he had given her enough space, and like it or not, he was going to call her tomorrow.

CHAPTER 16

"You're up early," Roxy said as Alyssa entered the kitchen.

"I couldn't sleep. I was up all night thinking again about Max. I've been praying since the other night, and though I have no clear answer, I can't stop thinking about him, so maybe that is my answer. I'm going to go see him and apologize this morning."

"Good for you." Roxy raised her mug of coffee in a mock salute.

"After some coffee, of course." Alyssa laughed as she filled her own mug and took a sip.

With the coffee finished and her outfit on, she stood in front of the mirror. Dark circles still ringed her eyes though they were lighter after her application of foundation. She didn't think Max would care, but she still wished they weren't there. It was her own fault, however. If she had trusted Max the first time, she wouldn't have lost sleep over it the last few days.

As she pulled up to Max's house, she wondered briefly if she should have called first. Maybe he would still be sleeping, or maybe he and Peyton would have gone out to breakfast. It was still early after all. Dismissing the negative vibes, Alyssa parked the car and walked up the pathway to the front door. Her finger paused but pressed the round doorbell.

Max opened the door a moment later. A genuine smile flashed across his face before it fell, and his eyes widened. His head turned to both sides as if looking for something. He looked... nervous. Was it because she caught him still in pajama pants?

His pants hung low on his waist and a white t-shirt stretched across his chest. Alyssa's eyes were drawn to his muscular chest before she caught herself and looked away.

"Sorry, I guess I should have called, but…" her voice trailed off as she caught movement behind Max. A woman with long brown hair padded down the hallway as if she owned the house.

Max, hearing the noise, turned to the woman and then back to Alyssa. At least he had the decency to look embarrassed. "It's not what you think, Alyssa." His head shook back and forth, as he said the words, as if that added an extra reason for her to believe him.

"I think a woman spent the night in your house." Alyssa nearly spat the words at him in her anger.

"Okay, it is what you think but nothing happened. I went out with Justin last night because it was his birthday and Amber was too drunk to tell me where she lived—"

"Amber? You remember her name? Well, I guess that is an improvement from the lady at the restaurant. What was her name again? I should have listened to her. I can't believe I spent the last few days losing sleep over not believing you, and then when I come to apologize, you have another woman here." Her words were rushing out like a waterfall, but she couldn't stop them. "Was I just another notch to put in your bedside then? Were you going to seduce me and then forget my name too?"

"That's not fair," he said, firing back at her. "First off, you haven't let me explain. Second, you haven't called all week or returned my calls. I didn't know if you were ever coming back." His posture had quickly shifted from nervous to agitated, and he seemed to fill the large doorframe.

The woman appeared behind Max and laid a hand on his arm. "I heard shouting. Is everything all right, Max?"

He glared at her as he brushed off her hand.

After she looked from Max to Alyssa, the woman disappeared again.

"So, you just jumped on the next train, huh?" Alyssa hated the caustic tone in her voice, but she couldn't turn it off.

His arms crossed as he leaned back onto the frame. "I was trying to be a gentleman. I couldn't leave her at the club, and as she passed out in my car, I had no way of knowing where she lived. I didn't really have another option, Alyssa."

"There's always another option, Max." His name felt like poison on her tongue now. "Here, I'll give you one more." She narrowed her eyes at him. "See anyone you want. I'm done. I should have known you couldn't really change." She turned and headed toward the car, tears pricking her eyes and blurring her vision.

"Maybe it's a good thing," he shot back. "You talk about love and forgiveness, but all I see is a stubborn woman who thinks she never makes mistakes."

"That's not true," Alyssa said, but even as the words left her mouth, she wondered if it was. She spared one final look at him before climbing in her car. He still stood in the doorway, shaking his head at her. Her hands were shaking as she buckled the seatbelt, but blissfully the tears waited until she pulled out of the drive before tumbling down her cheeks.

"I'm such a fool. Why did I think he could change?"

She said the words aloud, hoping for a sense of peace, but silence was all she received in return. Silence and the mocking reminder that she had been too angry to believe him when he tried to explain. Could it be possible that he was just being a gentleman? The woman had been fully dressed after all, but she could have put on her clothes before exiting the bedroom. And if he was just being a gentleman why even go out in the first place?

She had no answer by the time she pulled up to her apartment, but at least the tears had stopped for now.

"Whoa, that was short," Roxy said, pausing the show she was watching on TV when Alyssa entered. "What happened?"

Alyssa rolled her eyes as she slumped down beside Roxy. "There was a woman there who spent the night. He said it was innocent, but I don't believe him. I feel so stupid." At the last word, the tears sprung anew and began another slow trickle down her cheeks.

"Hey, it's not your fault. This guy has been playing the game for a while it sounds like. The only one to blame is him. I know what will make this better. Hang on." She bounded up from her chair and into the kitchen. Roxy had been a track star in high school and her long legs were still toned and in shape as she ran three miles every day.

There was the sound of cupboards opening and porcelain clinking, followed by the drawer and then the fridge opening and closing two times. A moment later, Roxy returned with two bowls of Chocolate Monkey ice cream.

"Ice cream? It's not even lunch time."

"Hey, ice cream makes everything better. It doesn't matter what time."

Alyssa smiled as she took the bowl, but though ice cream would make her feel better for the time it took to eat it, she knew it wasn't going to fill the aching spot inside her heart.

*M*ax sighed as Alyssa's car exited the drive. How had this gone so wrong so fast? Why hadn't she let him explain? He shut the door and trudged to the kitchen. Amber was perched on a barstool with a cup of coffee in her hand.

"I hope you don't mind that I helped myself to some coffee. I tried to ask, but you looked a little busy. Boy, this is quite the place you have here."

Her voice was too perky this early in the morning, and Max was already feeling grumpy after the argument with Alyssa. "Yeah, it's great."

"You seem angry. Is it about the woman at the door?" Her wide eyes were filled with curiosity but seemed to be lacking the knowledge of her part in his anger.

"Yes, it's about the woman at the door. She thinks I brought you home to... she thinks we…" He shook his head. "Anyway, it doesn't matter now. She left."

"Why didn't you just tell her that nothing happened?" She flicked her hand and took another sip of her mug. "I mean, I assume it didn't, since I woke up by myself and still in my clothes from the night before."

He stared at her, trying to contain his anger. "I tried telling her that, but unfortunately your poor timing didn't help matters."

Amber's head snapped back in surprise. "Well, excuse me. I had a pounding headache and needed some coffee. By the way, where's your aspirin?"

Rolling his eyes, he stepped over to the highest cabinet and pulled out a bottle of aspirin. He walked back to her and slammed it on the counter before returning to his room. He wanted this woman out of his house now, and as Peyton was still asleep, he needed Helen to come stay at the house in case she woke.

She showed up fifteen minutes later wearing what looked like a housecoat with curlers in her hair.

"You could have gotten dressed first," he said as he opened the door. A sliver of his anger fizzled at the sight of her.

"And risk your daughter seeing some strange woman

in the house? I think not. You should have let me take the girl home last night." She poked him in the chest as she stepped inside the house.

"Yeah, I should have," Max sighed. "Alyssa showed up to apologize, but then she saw Amber. She's furious this time, Helen. I don't think she will ever forgive me."

Helen had the decency not to say 'I told you so,' but she did shake her head sadly. "We'll figure something out, Max. For now, get that woman home."

Max nodded and marched back to the kitchen. "Let's go, Amber."

She jumped at his forceful voice, spilling coffee on the countertop. "Go? Where are we going?"

"I'm taking you home."

"Already, but I thought we could—" She stopped as he glared at her.

"You have cost me quite enough. We aren't going to do anything. Now, come on."

After another swig of whatever was left in her coffee mug, she set it on the countertop and slid off the barstool, following him out to the garage.

"Where to?" he asked her when they were both buckled.

"3410 Buckley Street."

Unfamiliar with that location, Max plugged it into his phone and sighed when the ETA showed half an hour drive.

"So, I guess this means you won't call me?" she asked when he pulled up in front of her place.

"Out." He pointed out the door, feeling a little mean, but also relieved he would never have to see her again, and he hadn't tried to trick her. He should have just called her a taxi, but in his effort to turn over a new leaf, he had thought taking her home was more gentlemanly. Now, he just wanted to get home.

She pouted her lip as she opened the door. "Fine."

After the tedious drive home, a cup of coffee called his name. The pattering of little feet echoed down the hall as he entered the house.

"Daddy, Helen's here. You going somewhere?" Peyton asked, running up to him.

Reaching down, he swung her into the air and situated her on his hip. "Nope, I'm staying home with you all day. Helen was just watching you while I took care of some business."

"Oh, good. Can we play princess today?" Her bright blue eyes shined back at him.

"I can't think of anything I'd rather do, but can you let me get some coffee and breakfast first?"

"Okay."

After he set her on the floor, she scurried into the living room to watch her favorite cartoon. Max turned to Helen. "What does playing princess involve?"

"Well, when I play with her, it involves a tiara and a

wand, but maybe she won't make you wear the tiara." Helen winked at him and smiled.

"Haha, very funny." Max grabbed a mug from the cupboard and filled it with coffee. Though the warm beverage calmed him, it did not heal the hole in his heart from Alyssa's departure. "What am I going to do, Helen?" he asked as he sank onto the barstool.

"First, you are going to eat breakfast." She placed a plate of pancakes and eggs in front of him. "Then, we are going to figure that out. Now eat up."

CHAPTER 17

"Where are you going?" Roxy leaned against the counter, her arms crossed and her eyebrow raised, as Alyssa wheeled a suitcase behind her into the kitchen.

"I'm going home. I need to get away from here for a few days, so I'm going to see my Aunt Sandra."

Roxy's head fell forward. "Are you sure? You haven't been back there since—"

"I know," Alyssa said, cutting her off. She hadn't been back home since her mom died a few years ago from cancer, but her conflicting emotions proved too much for her. She needed some clarity and her Aunt Sandra was the one person who had always been able to give her clarity. "But I'm hoping it will help, and it's only for a few days."

"I get that." Roxy pushed herself off the counter and crossed to Alyssa, enveloping her in a hug. "Have a safe trip, and I hope you find the answer you're looking for."

"Me too."

*A*s Alyssa pulled into Sandra's driveway, a feeling of peace enveloped her. Sandra wasn't her aunt by blood, but she had been her mother's best friend and had always been like a second mother to Alyssa. Now, Alyssa couldn't wait to see her. It had been too long, especially since Henry had passed away and all of their children were now out of the house. Sandra must be lonely, and Alyssa made a mental promise to visit more often.

Sandra opened the door before Alyssa could even knock. The smile on her face reached from ear to ear. "Alyssa, it's so good to see you."

She opened her arms and Alyssa dropped her suitcase, so she could lean down and hug the woman. "It's good to see you too, Aunt Sandra."

"Well, come in, come in. I've got chicken in the oven and a salad ready for dinner. You do still eat, don't you? You've gotten so skinny, I'm no longer sure."

"Yes, Aunt Sandra, I still eat. I've just been so busy

with school that I've been going non-stop, but I finished my last final last week, so I'll have time to slow down now." Alyssa set her suitcase just inside the door as she followed Sandra to the kitchen. She must be cooking her famous garlic chicken because the scent of garlic was strong in the air.

Alyssa watched as Sandra wheeled over to the modified counter and began tossing in the few remaining ingredients needed for the salad. "How did you do?"

"I did well. I got A's and B's on all my finals."

Dropping the wooden spoon she was using to stir the salad, Sandra turned her deep brown eyes on Alyssa. "Your mother would be so proud of you—is so proud of you as I know she's looking down on us."

Tears pricked Alyssa's eyes at the mention of her mom. "Thanks, Aunt Sandra. I just wish she could help me with finding a good man."

Sandra opened her mouth to speak but was interrupted by the doorbell. "Oh, that will be my friend Callie. Will you go let her in? I invited her over because you two are about the same age and she needed a night off. She's got a little one at home."

"Sure." Alyssa blinked as she headed back to the front door. Why would she invite someone else over? Alyssa had told her she wanted to talk, right?

On the other side of the door was a beautiful woman

with dark hair and green eyes. Her face lit up in a smile as she saw Alyssa. "You must be Alyssa. Sandra has told me so much about you. I'm Callie," she stuck out her hand, "and I'm so pleased to meet you."

"Uh, same," Alyssa stammered, shaking the outstretched hand, "though Aunt Sandra didn't tell me much about you."

"That's Sandra for you." Callie stepped into the living room and closed the door behind her. "I'm sure she has something planned. She always does. Called me up today and said you were coming and could use some sisters in Christ around you, so here I am." She leaned in and lowered her voice. "Plus, I needed a break."

Alyssa nodded though she had no idea what Callie was talking about. The only thing she was sure of was that her aunt had set this up, but she was not sure she'd feel comfortable telling a stranger about her issue."

"Sandra, can I help?" Callie had reached the kitchen ahead of her and was already grabbing glasses down from a cupboard.

"Just with what you're already doing. Here, Alyssa, take this to the table please." Sandra handed her the bowl of salad and Alyssa carried it to the table set for three.

"Tea or water?" Callie asked, setting a jar of sun tea on the table.

"Tea is fine," Alyssa responded watching Callie and

her aunt interact. They must get together often because Callie seemed to know where everything was in the kitchen.

"Sit, sit," Sandra said, wheeling over with the baked chicken in a dish on her lap. She set it on the table and motioned for Alyssa to sit.

Callie took the other chair, and the three women scooted up to the table. Sandra grabbed Alyssa's left and Callie's right hand in hers before bowing her head. "Lord, we are so thankful that Alyssa has come to visit. Be with us in this place and fill us with your wisdom as we tackle her problem. Bless this food and this company. In your name, Amen."

"Amen," Callie and Alyssa echoed, and the passing of the food began.

Alyssa hadn't expected to feel comfortable sharing her information with Callie, but as the dinner progressed, she saw why the two were friends. Callie appeared easy to talk to, and as she shared some of her past with Alyssa, Alyssa realized she might have a good perspective on the situation.

By the time dinner was over and the women had retired to the living room with cups of tea, Callie felt like an old friend, and Alyssa found herself sharing the whole ordeal with them both.

"It sounds like you might care for him," Sandra said as Alyssa finished.

"I care for Peyton," she said taking a sip of her tea, "He is just... I don't know what he is, besides frustrating."

Callie and her aunt shared a glance, and Alyssa wondered what unsaid words passed between them.

"I know he made some mistakes, but we all have," Sandra said. "Remember, we are all broken people and God can use us even broken as we are."

"I get that Aunt Sandra, but he had a woman there. What if it means he hasn't changed and he'll just keep doing the same thing? I don't want to get mixed up in that."

"People can change. I did. Your mom did. Callie did. It just takes someone showing them the love of Jesus." Her aunt looked down into her tea cup. "Darn. Empty. You two keep talking, I'm going to get a refill."

Had she shown Max the love of Jesus? The image of their last fight flashed through her mind, and Alyssa cringed. That was definitely not Jesus' love that day.

"I don't want to contradict what Sandra says," Callie's voice brought Alyssa back into the present. "She's probably the wisest woman I know, but I was with a man who couldn't change or wouldn't change. The thing is, if you do some soul searching, you'll know. I was blind at first, but when I really looked inside, I realized Daniel would never change, or at least not for me. I think if you look inside, you'll know whether this Max is capable of change or not."

"Thanks, Callie. I'm glad Sandra invited you over tonight."

"I am too," Callie said, returning the smile.

CHAPTER 18

"Why are we here?" Peyton asked, as Max unhooked her from the car seat.

"Well, Alyssa and I are in a bit of a fight. I thought it would be nice if we gave her some space, so this is Helen's church."

Max had been unsure when Helen first suggested the idea of changing churches. What if Peyton hated it? But as they approached the small white church, Max felt a sense of peace.

Helen was at the door waiting for them. "You made it." She gave Peyton a high five before turning to Max. "Come in. Let me introduce you around."

The thought sent ice water through Max's veins, but he followed her in anyway, Peyton's hand clasped in his.

"This is Pastor Bill."

Pastor Bill was an older man with grey at his temples. He wore a button-down shirt and some slacks but no tie, and he looked a little more relaxed than Max's images of typical pastors.

"Pastor Bill, this is my friend Max and his daughter Peyton." Helen made the introductions and then stepped back, smiling.

"Pleased to meet you, Max and you, Miss Peyton. I hope you enjoy the service."

"Oh, I'm sure he will," Helen jumped in before Max could speak. "I know we all do every week." She grabbed Max's arm and steered him to the right. "Let's check Peyton in, and then you can escort an older woman to her seat."

Max smiled as he looked down at her hand on his arm. It seemed that she was escorting him currently, and he knew she was quite capable of finding her seat herself, but he humored her. After dropping Peyton in the small Sunday school room, he led Helen back to the sanctuary, but she took over when he tried to snag a seat in the back row.

"Oh, no no no," she said, pulling him forward. "The best seats are toward the front."

"But I don't want to sit up front." His fear, though he'd never tell Helen, was that if he was up front, people would watch him and be able to tell that he was a faker and not a believer.

She ignored his protests and situated herself in the middle of the third aisle, patting the chair beside her. With a sigh, Max entered the row and took the seat. The music started shortly after, and Max was surprised by the upbeat music. He knew Helen was young for her age, but he hadn't expected her to like this type of music. Three guitars, a drummer, a keyboard, and a piano made up the band along with four singers out front.

When the music ended, Pastor Bill took the stage and Max found himself drawn to the message. It was all about Jesus meeting you where you are. Though Max hadn't considered religion much in his adult life, he remembered the few times his parents had taken him when he was young, and the message then was all about being perfect or going to Hell. It was one reason why he had avoided religion for so long, but here was a man saying he didn't have to be perfect to have a relationship with Jesus because a relationship with Jesus would change him. He wondered how it would change him? He already felt different just having Peyton in his life.

The sermon was still bouncing around in his head as he and Helen walked down the hall to get Peyton.

"Max, Helen, look I drew us." Peyton proudly waved a white paper with purple scribbles on it. "That's me and there's you, Helen, and there's Alyssa."

Max's heart tightened at the mention of Alyssa's name. Would she ever forgive him?

"Who is that up in the sky?" Helen pointed to the scribble near the top of the paper. "Is that Jesus?"

Peyton's face fell. "No, that's Mommy. She's on her way to see Jesus."

Max and Helen exchanged a glance before Max turned to Peyton. "Peyton, honey, your mom isn't going to see Jesus yet. She's just in New York."

"No, she's not." Peyton shook her head. "Jesus told me last night he was taking her but not to be scared."

Max wondered if Peyton was going crazy. Wouldn't he have gotten a call if Sarah had passed? He pulled out his phone, expecting nothing, but the little green phone icon had a number one floating to the upper right. He clicked on it and the voicemail loaded.

"Hello, Maxwell Banks? This is Dr. Steven Youngblood with Memorial Sloan Kettering Cancer Center in New York. You are listed as a contact for Sarah Moore, and I need you to call me right away."

Max lowered the phone before he heard the number, but he would listen to it again. Right now, his shock at Peyton's knowledge was more than he could take.

"Why don't I stop and grab some lunch and meet you at the house?" Helen suggested after seeing the look on Max's face.

"Sure, that sounds fine." He took Peyton's hand and headed to the parking lot. The walk there was silent, but as soon as she was strapped in the car, he turned to her. "How did you know, Peyton? About your mom?"

"I told you; Jesus told me. He said he had to take my mommy for now, but that he'd send me another mommy soon. He said you'd take care of me and be my daddy from now on. You will, won't you?" Her voice held no fear as she spoke about issues much bigger than herself.

"Of course I will, Peyton." The words constricted his heart though. He didn't know the first thing about being a dad permanently. He had failed miserably in his first few weeks, and without Alyssa, he didn't know how he'd get through it.

*A*lyssa was at lunch with Sandra and Callie's family when her phone rang. As she pulled it out and glanced at the caller ID, her heart filled with dread. With a New York area code, it was either Sarah or someone from the hospital, and she feared it was the latter as they had told her Sarah was too weak for phone calls when she had tried a few days ago.

"Hello?"

"Yes, can I speak with Alyssa Miller?"

The voice was masculine and the vice on her heart pulled tighter. "This is Alyssa."

Sandra and Callie both stopped conversing and stared at Alyssa.

"Alyssa, this is Dr. Steven Youngblood. I was treating Sarah Moore—"

"Was? Is she?" Alyssa couldn't bring herself to say the words, but she didn't have to.

"I'm sorry, Alyssa, her cancer was too advanced, and she passed away this morning."

Alyssa thought she had been prepared for this knowledge. After all, Sarah had been diagnosed nearly a year ago, and she had been at her appointment two months ago when the doctor told Sarah the cancer had progressed to a point that probably wasn't treatable. Memorial Sloan had been a last-ditch effort, but Alyssa had still held on to hope that God would perform a miracle.

She dropped her head in her hands as words failed her. Peyton! The little girl popped in her mind amid her grief. "Does Peyton know?"

"We tried to reach Maxwell Banks, but I was forced to leave a message, and he hasn't returned my call yet."

Maxwell. Of course, she would have to talk to Maxwell again. They would have to plan the funeral, and she needed to make sure Peyton was okay. His very name still dredged up feelings in her heart, but she was no longer sure if they were feelings of attraction or anger.

"Thank you, Dr. Youngblood. Is there anything else we need to do?" Her voice sounded strained to her ears, and her throat was quickly constricting with tears.

"I just need an address to send her belongings and the name of the mortuary you would like her transferred to as I'm assuming you would like her buried there."

Alyssa rattled off the information and managed to hang up the phone before the tears broke through the gates and flooded her cheeks.

"Alyssa, what's wrong?" her aunt asked, taking her hand.

With no voice, all she could do was shake her head and let the tears fall. Callie passed Hope to JD and huddled next to her, wrapping her arm around Alyssa for support.

When the tears finally tapered, Alyssa told them about Sarah.

"Oh, Alyssa, I'm so sorry," Sandra said. "First your mother and now this. I can't imagine how you must be feeling but remember that God can ease your burden. And so can talking to other believers. Don't shut this grief in."

"I have to get back. The doctor hadn't been able to reach Max. I don't even know if he knows or if he plans to keep Peyton."

"Would you like me to come with you?" Callie offered after shooting a quick glance at her husband.

Alyssa attempted a small smile. Callie had quickly become a friend in the short time she'd known her, but this was her battle. "No, I'll be fine, but thank you."

"We'll be here for you whenever you need us," Callie said, squeezing her arm.

After she was packed, Alyssa hit the road, playing over and over the words she would say when she saw Maxwell again.

CHAPTER 19

"I don't know what I'm going to do, Helen."

Max dropped his head into his hands. Peyton was napping, and Helen had stayed to listen to his fears.

"You'll do what we all do. You'll pick yourself up and become a great father. You're already getting better."

She placed a cup of tea in front of him, eliciting a small smile. He had come to enjoy these chats with her over tea.

"But what if I mess up?"

"You will, but we all do." She reached across the table and covered his hand with hers. "You apologize and you try to do better the next time. Peyton will understand, and believe me, she'd rather stay with you than be put into a house she doesn't know. Plus, you have something else on your side. You have the money to be able to take care of her and provide her with anything she might need."

Max took a sip of tea as he stared at the wise woman. If nothing else, he'd done something right to have her in his corner. "Thanks Helen, I don't know what I'd do without you."

"What about the rest of your family, Max?" Helen asked. "You never talk about them, but it might be time to introduce Peyton to them."

Max sighed. "I know. I've been thinking about that. My parents live here in the city, but we haven't spent time together in years, not since my brother moved to Scotland and they became believers. I was fresh out of college and thought I knew everything, you know?"

Helen nodded and motioned for him to continue.

"Anyway, they tried to push Jesus on me, probably hoping to save at least one of their wayward sons, but all it did was push me away. Then I met Justin and he introduced me to the party lifestyle. I thought it was filling the void in my life, but boy was I wrong. Needless to say, my lifestyle drove an even bigger wedge between us."

"You know my strength doesn't come from myself, right?" She took a sip of her tea and looked at him over the rim of the cup as if measuring his reaction. "It comes from my friends, my family, and trusting God to help me handle anything I can't."

"How long have you been a believer?" Max couldn't believe he was even asking the question, but the combination of the sermon, Peyton's dream, and Sarah's death had all been working in his head.

"Since I was ten. Of course, it was much easier then." She laughed wistfully, and her eyes glazed over as if she was remembering some fond memory. "I strayed for a time in college when I was trying to figure out my own way, but God saved me when I was at my lowest, and when I stopped fighting him and started listening, my life got simpler. Not easier, mind you. Following Jesus doesn't always mean an easy life, but simpler, and I knew he'd always be there for me."

"I'm not sure I'm ready for all that," Max said, twirling the cup around, "but could you tell me how in case I get there?"

"Of course." Helen smiled and began to lay out the simple steps to accept Jesus into his heart.

*A*lyssa inhaled deeply as she parked in front of the palatial house. Was she sure she wanted to do this? After all, it had only been a day since she left in anger. Somehow, she felt less angry now. The loss of

Sarah had put things into perspective and whatever happened between her and Max, she needed to be around for Peyton.

She was surprised when Helen opened the door. "Hi, Helen, I wasn't expecting to see you."

"Nor I to see you." She smiled and stepped outside, closing the door slightly behind her after sneaking a glance down the hallway. "However, I am glad you're here. I needed to speak with you."

"If it's about Sarah, I already know."

"It isn't. It's about Max."

Alyssa held up her hand. "Helen, I don't—"

"No, you're going to listen to me," Helen said, cutting her off. "Then you can make up your own mind with what I have to tell you."

Shocked by Helen's firm tone, Alyssa closed her mouth and nodded for her to continue.

"Thank you. Now, I know Max has a history, but he did not sleep with that woman who was here Saturday. I was here when he brought her home Friday night. He put her up in the guest room for the night. He tried to take her to her home, but she had passed out before he got her address. He was put in a bad situation, and he tried to do the right thing."

"Do you trust him?" Alyssa asked, her voice quiet.

"I've never seen a man make such a drastic change in such a short time, but I see the way he looks at Peyton and the way he looks at you, and I do trust him. He's been a wreck since you left Tuesday and even more yesterday at the thought of losing you. He will never be perfect, but his heart is open and he's asking questions about Jesus. I'm going to keep encouraging him, and it would help if you did too, but I'll leave that up to you. He's in the living room."

With that, Helen opened the door for her and waved goodbye as Alyssa stepped in.

"Alyssa?" Max's face registered his surprise as she entered the living room. "What are you doing here?"

"I came to see if you knew about Sarah. Dr. Youngblood said he couldn't reach you and had to leave a message. Does Peyton know?"

"She does. In fact, she knew before we got the call. She had a dream," he added, as her eyes widened in confusion.

"How is she doing? Is she okay?"

"She seems all right. She's napping now." He stood and crossed to Alyssa. "I'm glad you came, though. I didn't like the way we parted last time." His hands reached out to hers, and after a moment, she accepted, taking a step closer to him.

"I didn't either. I'm sorry I didn't trust you. There's been hurt in my past, and I have to admit your past frightens me, but I know you're trying."

"I promise to keep trying if you'll let me. I don't think I can do this with Peyton all on my own."

As he took another step closer, Alyssa could feel the heat radiating off him combining with the heat building inside her. Her breath caught as his fingers intertwined with hers and he pulled her closer. Was he going to kiss her? Did she want him to?

His eyes flickered back and forth between her eyes and her mouth before closing. His face began to lean down to hers, but before their lips could touch—

"Aunt Lyssa." Peyton's voice caused them both to jump back.

Heat seared across Alyssa's face. "Hey, Peyton. How are you doing?"

"I'm okay. I'm sad about Mommy, but Daddy said he wouldn't leave me."

A small smile crossed Max's mouth as Alyssa glanced at him. "That's so good, Peyton, and I'm going to make sure and be around for you too."

"Are you going to be my new mommy then?"

"Uh," Alyssa looked to Max for help in answering the question.

A sheepish grin covered his face. "Sorry, I didn't tell you all of her dream. I guess Jesus told her he'd be sending a new Mommy to her soon."

"Oh, well, um, I'd never want to replace your mommy, but I'll always be here for you." The words stumbled out of Alyssa's mouth as she tried to find the best way to answer Peyton's question without promising something she couldn't.

"Okay." Peyton shrugged and switched the subject. "Daddy, can I have a snack?"

Alyssa smiled at the shifting thoughts of a nearly four-year-old as Max headed to the pantry to get her some goldfish.

When Peyton was distracted with her snack, Alyssa grabbed Max's arm and pulled him to the opposite side of the kitchen. "We need to discuss funeral arrangements. They're shipping Sarah's body back, but we need to get a casket and a ceremony set up."

"Right." Max's eyes shifted back and forth. This topic was clearly uncomfortable for him. "I have no idea how to go about that, but I'll cover the costs."

"Sarah left a list of what she'd like, just in case," Alyssa said, laying a hand on his arm. "We just need to get together to get it all done."

"Okay, I'll leave work early tomorrow. We should probably get it organized soon."

"Probably." Alyssa sneaked a glance at Peyton. "I know she seems okay now, but it's going to be hard for her."

"Maybe you can stay tonight and teach me how to pray for her?"

Alyssa blinked at him. She didn't think he prayed.

"I went to Helen's church this morning," he said, smiling. "I really liked the preacher and his words have been cycling through my head all day. I'd like to start small, but I figure Peyton will need someone praying with her nightly now. Real prayers and not the half-baked ones I've been saying lately."

Alyssa nodded, tears pricking her eyes, but not from sadness this time. This time, they were tears of joy that Max appeared to be opening up his heart just as Helen had said.

CHAPTER 20

"Dude, sorry about not returning your call Friday night, but I was a little busy if you get my drift." Justin sat in the chair across from Max and wiggled his eyebrows for emphasis.

"Yeah, well, that little stunt nearly cost me something real, so I hope you enjoyed it as it's the last time I'll be going out." Max turned on his computer as he sat behind his desk. Though it appeared Alyssa had forgiven him, he was still miffed at Justin's behavior.

"Whoa, man, what do you mean? I heard you hooked up with Amber."

Max rolled his eyes. "No, I didn't hook up with Amber. I tried to take her home since you left her there, but she was so drunk that she passed out before I got her address. I ended up having to take her to my place, which is where Alyssa found her the next morning when she came to apologize. Needless to say, that didn't go well, and we'd probably still be fighting if it weren't for Sarah dying."

"Wait, what? Sarah's dead?"

"Yes, she passed away yesterday." Max bit his lip to keep the hurtful words in his mind from spilling out of his mouth. He shouldn't be judging Justin so harshly. He had been the same a few short weeks ago.

"So, what are you going to do with the girl?"

"The girl?" Max's head fell forward, his eyes wide. "You mean my daughter?" Hard as he tried, he couldn't keep the angry edge from creeping into his voice. "I'm going to raise her of course."

"Dude, that will totally put a cramp in your style."

Max shook his head sadly. "I don't think you understand that my style has changed. I don't want the playboy life anymore. I don't want a different woman every time. I want just one, and I want to be a good father to my daughter. She needs me, especially with her mom being gone now."

Justin blinked as if these concepts were completely foreign to him, and maybe they were. They had been foreign to Max before Peyton and Alyssa entered his life.

"Wow, I have no idea who you are anymore, man." Justin shook his head as his stood.

Max could try to explain, but he saw no need.

Suddenly, he had way less in common with Justin, and he didn't see their friendship lasting anyway.

With a final glance, Justin shook his head one more time and exited the office. Max sighed in relief.

The rest of the day passed uneventfully, and at two p.m., Max shut down his computer for the day. He was picking Alyssa up, so they could pick out a casket for Sarah.

"What do you think?" Alyssa asked, running her hand over a casket a dark mahogany color. "She always said she wanted simple, but I can't put her in that thing." She pointed to the bargain basement casket, which was just a step above a pine box.

Max couldn't imagine putting Sarah in there either. "Look, I have the money. Let's get a nice one. I want it to be something that doesn't scare Peyton as well."

Alyssa's eyes widened. "Oh, I hadn't even thought of that. Do you think she's old enough to go?"

"Whether she is or isn't, Sarah was her mother, and I think keeping her away would be a big mistake." Max recalled a childhood friend who lost his father in a motorcycle accident. He hadn't been allowed to attend the funeral, and he had carried a lot of hurt afterwards causing him to act out in school.

"You're right. I should have remembered that from my psychology courses."

"Hey, don't be hard on yourself. You have a lot you are dealing with right now."

Alyssa eyes filled with water. "I mean, I expected this. I thought I was prepared for this, but I'm not. Peyton needs a mother."

Max pulled her to his chest. She did not fight him but curled up under his chin. "Look, didn't you tell me that God will provide a way? That he's always there for you?"

She sniffled and looked up at him. "Yeah, but I didn't think you were listening."

He took her face in his hands. "I always listen when you speak. You are the most amazing woman I have ever known. You have this inner strength that shines through. This is hard, but God will show us what to do."

"Us?"

Max could hear the hope in the singular word. He paused for a moment as he reflected on the decision he made last night. After he had put Peyton to bed, the feeling that he needed to have Jesus in his life had pressed strongly on him, and he had sunk to his knees on the floor by his bed and prayed for Jesus to be his guide.

"Yes, us. I wanted that strength that you and Peyton

and Helen have. I wanted to be the father she needs, and I knew I was going to need help, so I prayed last night."

Alyssa's eyes widened. "You prayed? Like 'accepting Christ' prayed?"

A smile pulled at the corner of his lips. "Yes, like 'accepting Christ' prayed."

"Oh, Max, I'm so happy for you." She threw her arms around his neck and enveloped him in a hug. "Oh, sorry," she said, pulling back.

"Don't be sorry. I could get used to hugs like those. In fact, I hope you are happy for us. I'm hoping that you plan to stick around with Peyton and me."

Alyssa nodded, a smile on her face, and though he wanted more than anything to kiss her, Maxwell refrained because kissing her in a room full of caskets just seemed wrong. Instead, he squeezed her hand and pointed to the deep red casket.

"I think that is the one."

"I agree."

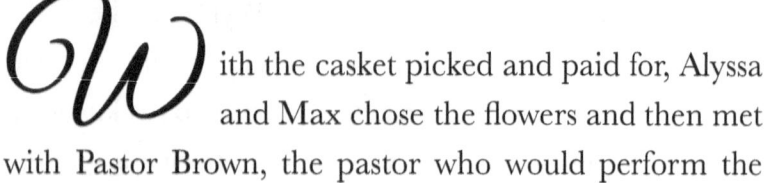

With the casket picked and paid for, Alyssa and Max chose the flowers and then met with Pastor Brown, the pastor who would perform the service.

"Here is what Sarah wrote down that she wanted

before she passed." Alyssa handed over the notebook sheet of paper, which the pastor took and scanned.

"We should be able to do this without a problem. Are you two planning on a Friday service?" He folded his hands together and looked from Alyssa to Max.

Alyssa looked to Max who nodded. "Yes, Friday should be fine with us."

With those preparations done, Max and Alyssa headed out to his car. She held tight to his arm, drawing strength from him. "Can I spend time with you and Peyton tonight? I don't think I can handle being alone."

"Of course you can. You know you are always welcome in my house."

The ride back was quiet, and Alyssa's mind wandered as the buildings passed by. It had been hard losing her mother to cancer, but it felt even harder losing Sarah. Maybe it was because of Peyton, but she thought it was more because of Max. Her heart was torn at the contrast of her joy of his acceptance of God and the feelings she knew were developing between them and the guilt that she felt being with him when Sarah couldn't.

"What are you thinking?" he asked finally, breaking the silence.

She turned to him, a small frown on her face. "I am struggling with my feelings. I am so sad at Sarah passing, but I'm so happy for you, for us, and it feels wrong."

"I know what you mean. I'm feeling the same thing,

but shouldn't we be happy that Sarah is no longer in pain?"

Alyssa shook her head. "How did you get so knowledgeable all of a sudden?"

"I had good teachers." He squeezed her hand with his free one. "It will get better."

Maxwell pulled into the garage and opened the door for Alyssa. Before stepping in the house, they both took a deep breath to try to clear their heads.

Helen, sensing their moods, hugged each of them before she left. "I'll be praying for all of you."

After the trio had dinner and Max put Peyton to bed, he joined Alyssa on the couch.

"Can you just hold me?" she asked as she scooted closer.

Max opened his arm and smiled as Alyssa scooted in. Her dark hair spilled across his chest and he couldn't keep from stroking the soft locks with his free hand. A flowery smell drifted up and tickled his nose. He wondered why he had never enjoyed this with the other women of his past. There was something comforting about having Alyssa's body curled up to his without expectation of anything else.

CHAPTER 21

"Where are we going, Daddy?" Peyton asked as he strapped her into the car seat.

"To meet my parents, Peyton. I think it's about time you met your grandma and grandpa. Would you like that?"

Her eyes lit up as she nodded.

Max laughed and tussled her hair. "Let's hope you still feel that way after meeting them," he said under his breath as he climbed into the driver's seat.

His mind replayed the phone conversation with his mother as he drove. He had called last night, not wanting to show up unannounced and have them not let him in. Though she had been excited to hear from him, there had been a distance in her voice. He hoped it was just cautionary on her part, but as he pulled into their driveway, his stomach clenched into knots. He hadn't told her about Peyton on the phone, and he had no idea how they would handle the situation.

Their house was a modest rambler on a few acres of land. After coming to Jesus, they had sold their mansion and moved into a smaller house, another thing Max hadn't understood then, but did now.

Gathering his courage, he sighed and parked the car. After unstrapping Peyton, he held her hand and approached the front door.

His mother opened the door before the doorbell chime had finished sounding. There were a few more strands of grey in her hair, but otherwise she looked as he remembered her. "Max." Her voice was warm and her smile genuine as she opened her arms. Then her eyes took in Peyton, and her arms dropped. "Well, hello, who's this?"

"Hi, Mom," he said. "This is Peyton, my daughter."

Though her eyes widened slightly, and she shot him a look that said she expected an explanation, her demeanor remained the same with Peyton. "Hello, Peyton. I'm your grandmother. Nancy."

"Hi." Though Peyton had a death grip on his pants' leg, she released one hand and raised it in a wave.

"Well, come in, come in. Peter will be so happy to see you."

She led them down a carpeted hallway into a spacious living room. His father sat in a brown recliner, reading a newspaper. As they entered the room, he lowered it and his eyebrow rose as he saw Peyton.

"Hi Dad," Max said as his father stood. "I'd like you to meet my daughter, Peyton."

Peyton managed another small wave as Peter kneeled to her eye level.

"It is very nice to meet you, Peyton. I'm Peter, but I guess you can call me Grandpa."

"Okay, Grandpa."

Though questions remained in their eyes, his parents refrained from asking them and turned to small talk. Peyton climbed on Maxwell's lap as he took a seat on the couch. His mother perched on the other chair in the room.

After half an hour, Peyton was asleep on his lap as he had hoped.

"So, tell us how you've been," his mother said when she noticed the cadence of Peyton's chest.

Max took a deep breath. "It's been a ride, that's for sure. You know how my life was going, but a month ago, a woman from my past showed up on my door with Peyton. I hadn't known about her, but I took her in to help her mother, who was sick. Sadly, her mother, Sarah, passed away this last weekend."

His mother gasped and covered her mouth.

"So, Peyton's mine for good. I thought you should meet her since she'll be in my life."

"Are you sure, Max? Raising a child isn't something to take on lightly," his father said, crossing his legs.

"I know, Dad, but Peyton doesn't have anyone else. Sarah's parents died in a car wreck when she was in college, and she was an only child. Besides, she's grown on me, and I can't imagine my life without her now. There's more, though."

His mother's hands bunched together as she waited for him to continue.

"I became a believer. Sarah was one and Peyton is too. So is the nanny I hired and Alyssa. Between all of them, they showed me what my life could be like, and I accepted him a few days ago."

Tears glistened in his father's eyes and streamed freely down his mother's cheeks.

"Oh, Max, we're so proud and so happy for you," she said, wiping away her tears.

"It's an answered prayer, Son. Praise the Lord, but who's Alyssa?"

Max smiled as he pictured her beautiful face. "Alyssa was Sarah's best friend. She has helped me the last month with Peyton and stolen my heart. I want you guys to meet her soon, but I wanted to see how it went with Peyton first."

"We'd be honored to meet her," his mother said.

"She must be a special woman if she managed to help turn your life around."

"She is. The funeral is on Friday, but how about we plan for the following week?"

"That would be great, and I hope you'll come over more often now."

Max smiled at his mother and the hope that colored her words. "I promise, Mom, but for now, I better get this monkey home and in her own bed."

He scooped his arm under Peyton and lifted her up. His mother and father stood and wrapped their arms around him. It felt good to have his parents back in his life.

🌼

The day of the funeral dawned before Maxwell was ready. The impending ceremony put a damper on the mood he had been feeling the rest of this week.

He reached for a black shirt and slid his arms inside before buttoning it up and tucking it into his black slacks. The monochromatic look matched his somber mood. He walked into the kitchen and started the coffee pot, enjoying the rhythmic dripping. *Lord, please help this day go as well as it can and give Peyton peace.*

Her tiny feet echoed in the kitchen a moment later. "Morning, Daddy."

"Morning, Bug. Did you sleep okay?"

"Yeah, but Jesus told me it was going to be a sad day. I have to say goodbye to Mommy. I don't want to say goodbye." Her eyes glistened with unshed tears.

Her perception and connection to Jesus still threw Max. Even though he had made the decision to give his life to Christ earlier this week, he couldn't say that he'd heard Jesus speak to him. "That's right Bug, but remember what we talked about? Mommy is no longer in pain."

"I know, but I... I miss her." The tears broke through the dam and rolled down her cheeks creating shiny iridescent tracks.

"Oh, Peyton." He enfolded her in a hug and let her cry against his shoulder. His heart broke for the pain she must be feeling. He had never understood women when they talked about hurting with their children and never wanting to see them hurt, but he understood it now. He would give anything to take her pain away.

When her sobs subsided, he grabbed her shoulders and stared into her eyes. "This is going to be a hard day, but I'll be there with you and so will Alyssa and Helen, okay? And none of us are going anywhere. We will be here with you whenever you need us."

She nodded and sniffled. "Okay, Daddy, I'll try to be brave."

Though Peyton didn't have a black dress, he managed to find a dark blue one that fit her. He helped her brush her hair and then heated up a waffle for her for breakfast. She sat at the table, coloring while she ate.

When breakfast was over, and her teeth were brushed, the two headed out to his car to pick up Alyssa. Helen had offered to meet them at the church.

Peyton's pink bear was clasped tightly to her chest in one hand and her drawing in the other as Max strapped her in, and he sniffed back his own tears threatening to spill over. She looked so small and helpless, and now he had to be the one to watch out for her.

When they arrived at Alyssa's apartment, Max texted her to let her know they were waiting. He would normally ring the bell, but he didn't want to leave Peyton in the car by herself. Alyssa appeared a moment later in a simple black dress. He could tell she was putting on her fake smile and her cheerful voice as she climbed in the car and greeted Peyton, but he could see the sadness in her eyes as well.

As soon as she turned around and buckled her seatbelt, he grabbed her hand and gave it a squeeze. She flashed him a tight smile before focusing out the window. He took no offense as he knew she was fighting tears herself.

The parking lot was full as they pulled up to the church. They had opted to have the funeral at Sarah's church in hopes it would be more comfortable for Peyton and because Sarah had many friends there. Helen had also offered to continue on to the gravesite afterward to make sure everything went smoothly there as well so that Peyton wouldn't have to sit through two ceremonies or see the hole in the ground.

Hand in hand, the trio entered the church, accepting consolatory wishes from everyone they passed. Peyton managed to keep a brave face on as they entered the sanctuary and took their places at the front.

As the pastor began to speak, Peyton climbed in Max's lap and curled her face into his chest. His arms circled her, offering the only measure of comfort he could at the moment. He sent up silent prayers for her peace. Alyssa scooted over and twisted toward Max, placing one hand on his shoulder and the other on Peyton's back. He shot her a grateful look before returning his focus to the ceremony.

When it was over, he asked Peyton if she wanted to see the casket, but she shook her head. "I want to remember Mommy from my dream, but can you give her this picture?" She held out the picture she had drawn that morning, which showed Sarah sitting on a cloud next to Jesus.

"I'll take it," Alyssa said.

Max nodded and took Peyton's hand, leading her to the back of the church as Alyssa stepped up to the casket. They had opted for a closed casket ceremony in case Peyton wanted to see the casket and Max was glad. He wanted to remember the way Sarah had looked when alive as well.

They followed the crowd to the kitchen where a small reception had been set up. People came over one at a time and in small groups to give their condolences. Helen found them and knelt in front of Peyton.

"You were such a brave girl in there. I'll have something special for you on Monday, okay?"

Peyton nodded and gave Helen a hug. "Thank you," Max mouthed to her as she stood.

Helen nodded and disappeared into the crowd. Alyssa appeared a moment later. "You know, I don't know about you, but I'm tired of being sad," she said. "Your mother had one final thing on her list and that was to take you to the zoo after the funeral, so how about it?"

Peyton's eyes lit up. "I love the zoo."

"I know you do, so what do you say?"

Peyton nodded and the three slipped out of the church.

The day had started overcast, but as the trio pushed open the front doors, a ray of sunlight broke through the clouds as if Sarah was smiling down on them. Alyssa grabbed Max's hand and smiled.

The zoo was mostly empty when they arrived. Peyton ran from one animal to the next, squealing in delight at each one.

"This was a good idea," Max said to Alyssa as they followed Peyton.

"Yeah, Sarah definitely thought ahead. She was really good at that."

"I wanted to ask if you would come have dinner with my parents next week," Max said as Peyton stopped in front of the giraffes.

Alyssa's eyes widened in mock surprise. "You have parents?"

"Haha, very funny." Max squeezed her hand and pulled her closer.

"Well, I was beginning to wonder. You never speak about them."

"We haven't had a very good relationship for a few years now, but we mended things a few days ago, and I'd like them to meet you."

"Then I would love to. I haven't been as close with my father either. After my mother died, we both processed her death differently, and he ended up remarrying."

"That's hard," Max said. "How long has your mom been gone?"

"Three years," Alyssa sighed. "Cancer took her too. I worry sometimes that it will take me as well."

"Hey now, you can't think like that. You aren't your mom or Sarah. Just because it happened to them doesn't mean it will happen to you. Besides, I'll be praying every day for your health. I need you around and Peyton does too."

Alyssa smiled and leaned into him as they watched Peyton wave at the giraffes.

CHAPTER 22

Though Max had told her not to stress, Alyssa couldn't stop the fluttering in her stomach at meeting his parents. What would they be like? Would they like her? What if they didn't?

"Will you stop?" Roxy asked. "You're making me nervous."

"What do you mean?" Alyssa hadn't voiced those questions out loud, had she? She thought they had just been in her head.

"You have crossed and uncrossed your legs seven times in the last minute, popped your knuckles three times, and bit your lip twice. You're emitting so much nervous energy that you're making my stomach bunch into knots and I'm not meeting anyone." Roxy finished her rant with a smile, letting Alyssa know that she was kidding. Mostly.

"I'm sorry. I just haven't done this in a long time, and Max and I are still new. I mean, are we even a couple? I don't think we've said as much."

Roxy shook her head. "Alyssa, if you haven't noticed the way that man looks at you, then you are crazy. You said yourself that he's changed from the playboy you met. That ought to tell you more than words ever could."

Alyssa took a deep breath and nodded. "You're right. I need to trust God and stop worrying on this one."

As if on cue, her phone beeped with the message that Max was in the parking lot. Normally, he would knock on the door, but as he had Peyton with him, they had agreed he would just text so as not to have to get her out just to strap her back in.

"That's my cue," she said, waving the phone. "Wish me luck."

"You don't need it," Roxy replied with a smile. "Knock 'em dead."

Alyssa flashed a grateful look at her friend before heading out the door. Max's Malibu was parked in the closest spot, and she slid into the seat, turning to say hello to Peyton.

"You get to meet my grandma and grandpa, Aunt

Lyssa." The pitch of Peyton's voice was so high it was almost a squeal.

"I know," Alyssa said with a smile and turned to Max. "She's not excited at all, is she?"

Max laughed. "Not one bit. Are you ready?"

Alyssa nodded, though the butterflies were still zooming in her stomach.

He squeezed her hand before pushing the gear shift to reverse and backing out of the parking spot.

Twenty minutes later, the car pulled into the driveway of a modest rambler. Alyssa blinked in surprise. Max's house was so much larger, and she had thought that at least some of his money came from his family.

"They downsized a few years ago when they became believers," Max said. "They said they didn't need to show off their money, they'd rather help people with it."

"I didn't. . ." Alyssa wondered how he knew what she had been thinking.

"Your eyes gave you away. They're expressive. Sometimes I don't think you know how much you say with them."

"I'll have to keep that in mind for the future." She should be embarrassed, but he was looking at her with such adoration that she found she didn't mind.

"Let's go," Peyton hollered from the backseat, lightening the mood and earning a chuckle from both Alyssa and Max.

"Yes ma'am," Max said, turning off the ignition and unbuckling his seatbelt.

Peyton was out a moment later and, hand in hand with Peyton in the middle, they stepped up to the front door. Max rang the bell and shot Alyssa a wink.

The door swung open a moment later, and a brunette woman with a few grey strands around her temple opened the door. She had the same piercing blue eyes as Max, and it was obvious she took care of herself from her slim figure and flawless skin.

"You must be Alyssa. I'm Nancy," she said, extending her hand.

"Yes ma'am. Nice to meet you." As Alyssa let go of Peyton's hand to shake Nancy's, Peyton broke free and rushed at Nancy.

"Grandma." She wrapped her arms around Nancy's legs and smiled up at her.

With a laugh, Nancy bent down and picked her up. "Come on in. We can get better acquainted inside."

Maxwell grasped Alyssa's hand as they stepped into the house together. She was grateful for the strength and comfort his touch gave her.

Nancy led them into a comfortable, homey kitchen. Tan cupboards lined the wall and complemented the grey and silver speckled marble counter and the stainless-steel appliances. A large dining table sat to the left surrounded by windows overlooking an immaculate backyard.

"Sit, sit." Nancy motioned to the dining table as she placed Peyton in a chair with a booster seat. "Peter, come and eat."

Peter, who Alyssa assumed was Max's father, entered the room. With the same dark hair and strong chin, she received a glimpse of what Max would look like in another twenty years.

"Hi, Dad," Max said, giving him a hug. "I'd like you to meet Alyssa."

"Ah, the girl who tamed the stallion. It's a pleasure to meet you."

He extended his hand and Alyssa shook it, blushing slightly at the title.

"It's a pleasure to meet you too, Sir."

"Please, call me Peter. Sir feels too formal."

"All right, Peter it is then." Alyssa smiled as she sat in the chair Max had pulled out for her. He squeezed her shoulder lightly after pushing her in, giving her a boost of positive energy.

Max took the chair to her right, and his father sat at the head of the table. Nancy placed a casserole dish and a salad in the middle of the table before taking her chair opposite Peter.

After a prayer, the food was passed around the table, everyone serving themselves. Alyssa enjoyed how comfortable the dinner was. It reminded her of dinners with her parents and Sandra and Henry before her mother passed.

When the dinner was finished, she offered to help Nancy clear the table. As Max, Peter, and Peyton headed into the living room, Nancy turned to Alyssa.

"I want to thank you. Even though we prayed nightly, we thought Max was going to be adrift forever. I don't know how you did it, but I can't thank you enough for bringing my son back to me."

Alyssa smiled and clasped Nancy's hand. "I didn't do anything. That was all God, but I am glad to see him changing too. He is such a different man now from the one I first met."

"I don't know how you stuck around, but I'm glad you did."

"Well, that you can thank Peyton for. I promised Sarah that I would look after her and make sure Max didn't screw up too badly. As much as he infuriated me in the beginning, I stayed for that little angel."

"She is that indeed," his mother said with a smile.

The two continued to converse as they cleared away the plates, and by the time Alyssa left that evening, she felt like she had known Nancy and Peter for years instead of hours.

"Your parents are pretty amazing," she said to Max on the drive back to his place.

"Yeah, they are. I'm glad I got to realize that." He flashed her a quick smile before returning his gaze to the road.

"Me too." There was a completeness in Alyssa's heart as they drove back, and she found she couldn't wait to see what the future held.

CHAPTER 23

Two Months Later

Max held the shiny ring in his hand and tilted it back and forth. The light glinted off the diamond, sending rainbow arcs across the wall. He couldn't believe he was thinking of purchasing this. Three months felt fast to be getting engaged, but he couldn't imagine his life without Alyssa in it and he didn't want to.

After the funeral, he and Alyssa had spent nearly every evening together. She took a job interning for a local therapist, but would drop by for dinner afterwards and stay for a few hours. They did devotionals together each night with Peyton before putting her to bed, and they made Helen's church their new home. Peyton didn't want to return to Sarah's church after the funeral, and Max liked Helen's better anyway.

Most evenings were pleasant, but Peyton still had a few days where she would cry for Sarah. Those were the hard days, but the day Alyssa brought over Sarah's belongings, including a photo album of her and Peyton and a sweater that Sarah always used to wear, Max had the idea to get a locket made for Peyton with a picture of Sarah inside. After that, whenever Peyton would get sad, she would curl up in the sweater and stare at the picture in the locket. It wasn't a perfect system, but it seemed to work for Peyton.

"What do you think?" the salesman asked as Max turned the ring one more time.

"I think it's perfect."

With the ring nestled in a black box and tucked away in his pocket, Max headed back to work. Now, he simply needed the perfect time and the perfect place.

"*D*o you have it all set up?" Helen asked as she gathered her items. Max had filled her in on the plan as soon as he got home.

"Yes, the dinner is Friday evening. Alyssa has already agreed to go. We'll start at six p.m., so I figure we'll be ready for dessert around seven. Will you be able to get Peyton there?"

"Of course, dearie. There is nothing in the world I would like more than to see you settled down."

Max shook his head and smiled at her good-natured ribbing, though he knew there was an element of truth there as well. Helen had been his biggest encourager from the beginning, and she would have been devastated if he had slipped back into his previous lifestyle.

"Okay, then I guess we're all set. I have to admit I'm a little nervous though. What if she says no?" Max had been wanting to ask her since just after the funeral—losing Sarah had brought home how short life could be—but it had always felt too soon. It still felt too soon, not for him, but he was afraid it would for Alyssa. Had he changed enough to thoroughly convince her he was no longer the guy looking for one good night, but instead was looking for a good lifetime?

Helen shook her head. "There's no way that woman will say no. She loves you just as much as you love her even if you two have been too stubborn to say it."

"I hope you're right." Max pulled her in for a quick hug before she left for the day and he turned all his attention on Peyton.

He hadn't told her his intentions yet because she was terrible at keeping a secret, but he didn't think she would mind having Alyssa around full time.

When Friday evening rolled around, Max logged out of his computer an hour early. In order for Peyton to participate in the dinner festivity before it got too late, he had opted for an earlier dinner. Though this meant a shorter workday, he had worked through lunch in order to not have anything hanging over his head during the weekend.

Before he could fully escape his office though, Justin popped his head in. Max hadn't seen much of him in the last month as he became more vocal about his faith and unwilling to support Justin's lifestyle.

"Hey, man, do you have a minute?" The serious tone in Justin's voice caught his attention and though he didn't really have a minute to spare, he nodded and motioned him in.

Justin closed the door, another odd thing for him, and crossed to the chair. He sat but didn't look up.

Max wanted to tell him to spit it out, but he could see that something heavy was weighing on Justin.

"You've been praying, man, right?" The words were muffled as his face was focused on the floor.

"Yeah, I've been praying." Max set down his satchel and mug and moved to the front of the desk. "What's going on?"

Justin looked up, fear and anger fighting for control

in his eyes. "I, um, just got back from the doctor's office. I've got an STD."

Max's knees gave out and he leaned against the desk. "Oh, man. I'm so sorry. Of course, I'll pray for you." As he said it, Max couldn't help but send up a grateful prayer that his life hadn't turned out the same way. He had gotten tested after Sarah's funeral partly because he was worried about not being there for Peyton and partly because he wanted to be sure he was offering Alyssa something worthy when it was finally time. "Is it the big one?"

"It's not HIV, but it's nearly as bad. I always thought pregnancy was the worst that could happen, you know?"

Max knew only too well. Though he had received the sex education talk in high school and knew all about STDs, he, like Justin, had thought he was invincible, that he was only seeing clean women, but when you didn't take the time to get to know them, it became harder to stay clean.

"I think this may be your wake-up call." Max worked to keep his tone even and non-judgmental. "Mine came when Sarah died. I realized my life had to change so I would be around for Peyton. Maybe it's time you take stock too and figure out what's really important to you."

Justin looked up but said nothing. Max took that as his cue and placed his hand on Justin's shoulder, closing his eyes and opening up his heart. "Lord, my friend

Justin is hurting. Please give him peace and insight into how to handle this problem. Forgive us our past sins and help us to follow the path you want us to be on. Amen."

"That's it?" Justin asked.

"That's it," Max said, smiling. "God knows what's in our heart, so the words aren't as important as the intention. Besides, nowhere in the Bible does it say we should pray long, flowery prayers. It just says to pray unceasingly, but this prayer isn't a cure-all. It isn't going to make your problem go away, and you'll have to decide if you want to make the life change, but if you do, you are always welcome to come to church with Alyssa, Peyton, and me. We'd love to have you with us."

"You're still with that girl?"

"Yep, in fact, I'm asking her to marry me tonight." Max pulled the black box out of his pocket and opened it up.

Justin shook his head. "Wow, I never thought I'd see the day. Maxwell Banks officially off the market for good."

"And happier than I've ever been," Maxwell said softly. "I think you could be too if you gave up this lifestyle."

Justin pulled his shoulders back and put his hands on his knees. "I'll think about it, but, uh, thanks for the prayer man."

Max's heart was heavy as he watched Justin leave.

He had hoped Justin would see the light, that a scare like this one would be enough to cause him to re-evaluate, but it looked as though Justin was more stubborn than Max thought.

Unable to do anything further now, Max gave the matter to God and gathered his things again. He'd have to take a quick shower in order to pick Alyssa up on time.

Once home, he gave Peyton a hug, promising to talk more once he was dressed. Then he jumped in the shower, letting the warm water calm his nerves.

After drying off, he picked out a blue shirt that brought out his eyes and tucked it into his black slacks. He decided to let his hair air dry to give it that tousled look. Before leaving the bedroom, he grabbed the black box from his work pants and shoved it in his left pocket.

"Wow, Daddy, you're handsome," Peyton said as he entered the kitchen.

"Thank you, Bug." He planted a kiss on her forehead. "Tonight is a special night. I'm going to ask Alyssa to marry me."

Her eyes grew wide. "You mean, she'll be my new mom?"

"If all goes well," Max said with a laugh. "And you get to help. Helen is going to bring you to dinner tonight and you are going to bring this box in,"–he pulled it out of his pocket — "and ask Alyssa to marry us. Can you try that for me?"

"What's in the box?" Her small finger reached out to touch the black velvet.

Max opened the lid and enjoyed the delighted surprise that spread across her face.

"It's so pretty."

"Yes, it is, so you have to be very careful with it. Now, do you remember what you're going to say?"

Peyton nodded, her eyes still large. "Aunt Lyssa, will you marry us?"

"Perfect," Max said, ruffling her hair. "I'm going to let Helen hold this ring until it's time, okay?"

Peyton's smile turned down into a small pout. "Daddy, I'll be careful."

"I'm sure you will, but I'll feel better if Helen has it until it's time." He looked to Helen, who nodded.

"I know exactly what to do. Don't you worry your pretty head," she said.

"Right." He handed her the box, holding it just a moment longer than necessary. His hope was that this proposal would dispel any lingering fears Alyssa might have but letting the ring out of his sight was way out of his comfort zone.

"We'll see you at seven," Helen said, tucking the box in her purse.

"*W*hat is the matter with you?" Alyssa asked as the waitress sat them. "You seem jumpy and distracted."

"Oh, just a hard day at work." It was not exactly a lie as the information Justin had shared still weighed on his mind.

"Do you want to talk about it?" The therapist in Alyssa began to show as she folded her hands together on the tabletop and regarded him.

"I do, but it's not dinner talk, so let's do it later." He reached across to grab one of her hands. "Why don't you tell me about your day?"

Alyssa narrowed her eyes at him but began to fill him in on her day. Of course, she couldn't discuss actual patients, so it was more about what she was learning by sitting in on sessions.

"Welcome to Se'bon, I'll be your waitress, Tamara. Our special tonight is—" She stopped suddenly, and Max looked up, his heart dropping into his stomach. "Maxwell? Maxwell Banks?"

Max nodded. This couldn't be happening again. Not tonight. "Hi, Tamara."

As Alyssa looked from the red-headed waitress to Max, he felt her hand tighten its grip on his.

"Well, I certainly never thought I'd see you again."

Tamara's voice had lost all friendliness and now dripped with venom. "I see you got a new flavor of the month."

"It's not like that," Max protested. "I'm sorry for what I did to you, but I've changed. I've been seeing Alyssa for months."

Tamara flashed Alyssa a cursory glance. "What does she have that I didn't?"

"God," Max stated simply.

Tamara's head dropped forward, and she looked at him like he had two heads. "I'm sorry, did you say God?"

"I did. Alyssa showed me what a relationship with Jesus was about, and I realized that my behavior was because I was missing something in my life, something I thought women could satisfy, but it turns out only God can."

Tamara rolled her eyes. "Whatever. I'm not waiting on you, but I'll get you another waiter."

As she spun and walked off, Max turned to Alyssa, ready to plead his case yet again. "I'm so sorry," he began.

"Stop," she said, shaking her head. A small smile played at her mouth. "I'm proud of you. You shared your faith tonight. That's not something you would have done a few months ago."

"But the reminder…"

"The past is the past, remember?" She squeezed his

hand, filling him with assurance. "Yes, it's unfortunate that this will probably keep happening for a time, but I knew that going in, okay?"

Max swallowed the emotion in his throat. "I don't know what I ever did to deserve you, but I love you, Alyssa Miller."

"I love you too."

Max almost wished he had the ring with him to propose right then. Instead, a male waiter with dark hair appeared at their table.

"My name is Pierre. Our special tonight is coq au vin paired with seared vegetables and a pomme puree. Would you like another moment?"

"No, I think we're good," Max said after glancing at Alyssa.

"Very well then, for the mademoiselle?"

"I'll have the special," Alyssa replied.

"And for the monsieur?"

"The same and a bottle of your best red."

Pierre nodded and glided away.

"Is it another special occasion?" Alyssa asked.

Max kicked himself. He knew Alyssa only drank on special occasions. He would have to make up something quickly to ease her suspicion. "It is, but it's a work thing. I want tonight to be about us, so I'll tell you later, okay?"

"Sounds intriguing," she said with a raised eyebrow, but thankfully she didn't push the subject.

The waiter returned a moment later with their bottle of wine and salads. Max's heart beat faster with each passing moment. He stole furtive glances at his watch whenever he thought Alyssa wasn't watching.

Finally, it was time for dessert. As they ordered a chocolate mousse, Max spared one final glance at his watch. Five till seven. His throat dried, and he swallowed repeatedly before picking up his glass and taking a large swig.

"Are you sure you're alright?" Alyssa asked. "You're acting weird."

He cleared his throat. "I'm fine. Just a tickle."

"Okay, if you say... Max, what is Peyton doing here?" Her eyes had left his and were focused over his left shoulder.

He turned and sure enough Peyton was meandering through the crowd waving at the other patrons. Helen followed behind her, smiling and shaking her head.

"Peyton, is everything okay?" Alyssa asked when she reached their table.

"Oh yes, Aunt Lyssa. I just needed to ask you something." She turned to Helen. "Can I have it now? She wouldn't let me hold it, Daddy."

"It's okay, Bug," Max said, smiling.

Helen handed over the black box discreetly and Peyton covered it with both her hands before turning back to Alyssa.

"Aunt Lyssa, will you marry me? I mean us." She opened her hands and held out the black box.

A gasp escaped Alyssa's mouth as she turned to Max. "Is this the special occasion?"

Max shrugged. "It is pretty special. I mean, if you'll say yes."

"Open it," Peyton shouted.

Alyssa opened the box and her eyes widened even further. "Max, I…"

Max's heart dropped at her pause. Was it too early? Was the ring too big?

"Of course, I'll marry you."

"Yay!" Peyton's loud voice and clapping drew the attention of the other patrons who also joined in clapping.

Max rose from his chair and pulled Alyssa up, wrapping his arms around her waist and twirling her lightly in a circle. "You've made me the happiest man alive," he said as he stopped the spin and placed his lips lightly on hers.

Another cheer erupted from the surrounding patrons and Alyssa pulled back, her face red. Peyton hugged her next and, after Alyssa sat back down, climbed up in her lap.

The waiter appeared a moment later with the dessert.

"Can we get two more chairs?" Max asked. "And another one of these to share?"

"Of course, Sir. I'll be right back." He placed the mousse on the table and turned, returning moments later with two more chairs.

"Sit," Max motioned to Helen. "Join us."

Peyton had already picked up a fork and begun digging into the mousse, but no one seemed to mind. Smiles were shared across the table, and Max knew this was a night he would never forget.

CHAPTER 24

"*D*o you have everything ready?" Aunt Sandra asked. She and Callie had come up a week early to help with the final preparations for the wedding.

"I think so," Alyssa said. She began to list everything on her fingers. "Catering, cake, flowers, venue, dress. Those are all done. I still need to get Peyton's flower girl dress and a dress for you, Callie, and my roommate, Roxy." She glanced down at her watch. "She should be arriving any minute."

As if she had heard Alyssa's statement, Roxy hurried over to them out of breath. "Sorry, I was helping Justin get his tux, and I lost track of time."

"Uh-huh." Alyssa smiled at her friend. Shortly after her engagement, Justin had begun attending church with them. His conversion had been even faster than Max's, though she attributed his STD scare to that. A few weeks later, Roxy had approached Alyssa as she finished up the invitations.

"Do you have 'find Roxy a new roommate' on that list?"

Alyssa jumped at Roxy's voice and looked up. "You'll be fine. You've always been so self-sufficient, but I'll help you look for sure."

Roxy pulled out a chair and sat next to Alyssa at the table. "Actually, I'm not sure I will be. I've never said anything, but you've kind of been my moral compass. I know I don't believe like you do, but I think I've changed for the better just being around you."

Alyssa was speechless for a moment. Though she'd been praying for years to reach Roxy, she had never any sign she was making a difference. "Well, I'll still be in town and you'll be welcome at our house any time." She paused at the mention of the word 'our.' It felt odd but nice on her tongue. "You could also come to church with us. In fact, this week would be a great week to come. Max's friend Justin has just started attending too.

Roxy's brow wrinkled. "Wait, Justin, isn't he the one you said gave you the creeps?"

A laugh escaped Alyssa's lips as she nodded. "One and the same. I guess something made him see the error of his ways, and he's thinking of changing course." She, of course, knew exactly what the something was as Max had brought it up in one of their nightly devotionals, but it was not her place to share the news, so she kept it to herself.

"So, your God has not only managed to change Max, but possibly his buddy Justin too?"

"I guess so." Alyssa had never thought about it that way, but she could see how an unbeliever might see it like that.

"Hmm, okay." Roxy shrugged, as if that answered her question.

"Okay, what?" Alyssa asked, confused.

"Okay, I'll go with you to church."

Alyssa was flabbergasted. She had never thought this day would come, and now both Justin and Roxy were planning on attending church with them. "I'll tell Max we'll meet him there this week then."

"Cool. I'm gonna go run." With that, Roxy got up from the table and grabbed her keys before heading out the door.

Alyssa stared after her. "Lord, I don't know what that was, but thank you." Her words were quiet, almost a whisper.

The attraction between Roxy and Justin had been evident from their first meeting, and while both Max and Alyssa had worried that Justin would slip back into his old ways, he hadn't so far. Even Roxy, who, while not as active as Justin, had been with her fair share of men through her relationships over the years, had agreed to try waiting this time around.

Alyssa couldn't be prouder of her friend or happier that the two seemed to be growing together in Christ.

"Well, now that you're here, I'd like you to meet my friend Callie and my Aunt Sandra."

Roxy waved to the women. "Hi, I'm Roxy."

"Good, now that that's out of the way, let's pick your dresses. Max gave me the gold card, so money is no object today."

Alyssa smiled as she fingered the gold card in her purse. Though her mom's family had money, Raquel had tried to raise Alyssa more modestly and, after her death, Alyssa hadn't been as close to her grandparents, so she was glad not to have to ask them for money. Besides, Max had insisted on purchasing them as a wedding gift to her.

The women headed to the back of the store where the bridesmaid dresses were kept. She and Max had decided on a color scheme of pastel pink and blue, but Alyssa hadn't wanted to force the women into one particular dress, so she had opted to let them pick their dress as long as it matched the colors.

Callie and Roxy went to work flipping through dresses while her aunt and Alyssa looked at flower girl dresses.

"I think this one is perfect," Alyssa said, holding up a pastel pink dress with rosettes across the front.

"It is beautiful," Sandra agreed.

With that task done, they turned their attention to

Callie who was modeling a simple pink number in front of the three mirrors.

"What do you think?" Callie asked.

"I love it," Alyssa said, and Sandra agreed.

Roxy stepped out of the dressing room a moment later in a powder blue empire waist gown. "Will this do?"

"It looks great." Alyssa couldn't believe how easy this process had been. She had been expecting it to take hours to find the perfect dress.

"So, who is Maxwell's other groomsman?" Callie asked after changing back into her street clothes.

"His brother. I've never met him because he lives in Scotland—he's a photographer—but I guess he's flying over for the wedding."

"Should be fun," Callie said, as they headed to the checkout.

*A*s the morning of the wedding dawned, Alyssa's stomach fluttered as if a swarm of butterflies were playing tag inside it. She had slowly been moving her items over to Max's, so all that was left were the clothes she planned to wear today and her shower items. The bed she was leaving for Roxy in case she wanted to forgo a roommate and make it a guest room.

A bittersweet feeling descended as she looked around the room she had called home for the last three years. It wasn't that she'd miss the room exactly, but she would miss the camaraderie with Roxy—the late-night ice cream binges and movie nights. Though she and Roxy planned to stay friends, she knew it would be different.

She grabbed the lone shirt still hanging in the closet and pulled it over her head. A pair of sweats were folded on the end of her bed, and she slipped into those as well. Her wedding dress was in a dress bag on the couch as she would change into it at the church after her hair appointment.

Roxy was at the table as Alyssa entered the kitchen. "You ready for your big day?"

"I think so. I'm nervous though." A pang of grief hit her as she added, "I wish my mom was here."

Pushing the sadness aside, Alyssa grabbed a plate and helped herself to the left-over eggs and bacon in the skillet. She set the plate on the table and poured herself a cup of coffee with creamer.

As she prayed over her food, she found her mind wandering to other prayers. She prayed for the day and for Stewart, Maxwell's brother. Though they had seemed happy to see each other, she could tell there was something else going on between them. She prayed for her father who was supposed to have arrived last night, but she still hadn't heard from him. They hadn't been super close since her mother died and last year he had remarried himself, which distanced them even further.

After breakfast, Alyssa packed up the last of her remaining items and took a final look around before following Roxy out to the car.

❀

*W*ith her hair done and her makeup fixed, Alyssa entered the church behind Roxy, Callie, and Sandra. They had been given a small office on the left side of the church to change in while the men had another small room on the right side.

Shortly after hanging her dress and unzipping the bag, a knock sounded at the door and Peyton peeked her head in.

"Hi, Peyton." Alyssa opened her arms and Peyton ran into them. "You look beautiful."

Max had done a good job getting her in the dress and keeping her clean before the ceremony, but her hair lay flat on her head.

"I'm on it," Roxy said, reading her mind and extracting the curling iron from her bag. Roxy had thought ahead and packed a curling iron, blow dryer, extra hose, and makeup in her bag just in case.

As Roxy began curling Peyton's hair, Alyssa pulled out the dress and slipped it on. She opted for something simple, so the dress was an unpretentious white shift that pooled on the floor. A delicate lace beading covered the bodice and a satin belt connected the bodice to the creamy white skirt.

Lifting up the skirt, she stepped into the Cinderella shoes she had bought. They weren't real glass slippers, but they were see-through, so they looked like them. Cinderella had been her favorite fairy tale growing up, and she and her mother had often discussed the glass slippers she would wear when she married. As her mother wasn't here to share the joy, Alyssa had made sure to have something that made her feel close to her. She blinked back tears as she remembered the many conversations with her mother.

"She's watching from Heaven," Sandra said, noticing the shine in her eyes.

"I know; it's just hard on days like this." Alyssa sniffed and pulled back her shoulders, determined not to cry out of sadness on the happiest day of her life.

Twenty minutes later, the rest of the girls were ready, and they led the way down the hallway. Helen stood outside of the sanctuary doors manning the guest book table, which also held their bouquets. She smiled at Alyssa and waved to Peyton as the girls grabbed their flowers and Alyssa handed the basket of petals to Peyton.

"Now, just like we practiced, remember? Small handfuls as you walk down the aisle."

Peyton nodded, her face focused and serious. "I have it, Aunt Lyssa."

"You look beautiful."

Alyssa turned at the voice of her father and smiled. "Hi Dad." She had been worried he wouldn't make it, but with him here, her shoulders felt lighter.

The music started, and Helen and Aunt Sandra made their way inside after one last hug.

Stewart appeared a moment later and escorted Callie in. Then Justin showed up to lead Roxy down the aisle. Peyton went next, and Alyssa smiled as she watched her through the cracked door. Peyton was not only dropping the flower petals but waving at each person she passed.

"I'm so proud of you, and I know your mother is too," Alyssa's father said as the music changed to the wedding march.

"Thanks, Dad. I'm so glad you could make it."

He squeezed her hand as she placed it on his arm. "I wouldn't have missed it for the world."

As he opened the door, Alyssa's eyes scanned the room and landed on Max. His smile was a beacon of light and like a tractor beam, she felt locked in his gaze. The connection never broke as she stepped forward.

When she reached the front, she hugged her father and handed her bouquet to Roxy before taking the final step to stand in front of Max. He grabbed her hands and a feeling of warmth and security surged down her arms.

"Dearly beloved we are gathered here today to join this man and this woman in holy matrimony."

As Pastor Bill began to speak, Alyssa's mind focused solely on Max, tuning out everything else around her.

*M*ax couldn't believe how lucky he was as he held Alyssa's hands and stared into her beautiful eyes. His life was now so different from where it had been going a year ago, but it was better than he ever would have imagined. His faith in God had rekindled his relationship with his parents and even his brother had made the trip to see his wedding. Now, if he could just reach Stewart, but that was a thought for another day.

Before he knew it, it was time to slide the ring on Alyssa's finger. He turned to get it from Justin and smiled at his friend. He had thought when he became a believer that their friendship wouldn't last, but instead it had inspired Justin to become a believer too and change his life as well.

"With this ring, I thee wed." The words were like lightning as he slid the ring on her finger. He felt a sense of security in his soul and knew he would never forget this feeling.

"With this ring, I thee wed," Alyssa said, sliding the gold band on his hand.

He had thought it would feel funny, like an anchor dragging him down, but it was light and liberating.

"I now pronounce you husband and wife. You may kiss the bride."

Max smiled as he leaned in and placed his lips on Alyssa's. It had been hard waiting to be intimate with her, but he knew tonight the relationship they shared would be more special than any of his other nights combined.

As the crowd cheered, he grabbed Alyssa's hand and they ran down the aisle and out of the sanctuary. The wedding planner had set up another room for them to go to directly after leaving until it was time to enter the reception and he led her there now. She was laughing as she ran beside him, one hand holding his and the other lifting the front of her skirt, so she didn't trip.

He opened the door and shut it behind them. Alyssa collapsed on one of the chairs in the room.

"That was fun, but I wish you had told me you planned on running. I did not wear my marathon shoes." She held up her feet and wiggled them, showing off the see-through Cinderella-esque heels.

"I promise I won't make you run again, at least not

242 | LORANA HOOPES

until you get better shoes." He pulled her to her feet and wrapped his arms around her waist. Her arms wound around his neck, bringing her body closer to his. He could almost feel her heart beating against his chest. "I am so glad I met you and that you agreed to marry me."

"Me too," she said with a smile, "though I'd have never believed it if someone had told me the first day."

He laughed as he shook his head. "I was so clueless."

"And helpless," she added.

"But we make a good team," he finished.

She nodded and parted her lips as she looked up at him. They were perfect and pink, and he needed to feel them again. Closing his eyes, he lowered his head until his lips were on hers. Though the kiss started slow, he could feel a raw need, a passion boiling inside. He knew if he didn't stop this soon they wouldn't make it to the reception.

Begrudgingly, he pulled back, breaking the connection. "We better go greet our guests."

Alyssa sighed, but nodded and followed him out of the room and down the hallway.

The church had a large room with an attached kitchen which was where Max and Alyssa had decided to have the reception, so people wouldn't have to drive to two places.

As they entered the room, a large cheer went up and

the DJ announced them over the speakers. "Mr. and Mrs. Maxwell Banks."

Max blinked and shook his head. He would have never thought there would be a Mrs. Banks.

"Daddy, Mommy." Peyton ran at them, a blur of pink as her little legs pumped.

Max swung her into his arms, placing a kiss on her cheek. "You were wonderful, Peyton. You tossed those petals like a pro."

"And waved, did you see me wave?" she asked, her head bouncing up and down.

"Future Miss America right here."

"Are we a real family now?" she asked.

"Yes, Peyton. We're a real family," Alyssa said. "I'll be there every night to tuck you in and I'll be there when you wake up."

Peyton reached out her other arm, enveloping Alyssa's neck and creating a hug triangle between the three of them. Max couldn't remember a time he'd been happier.

The End!

*I*f you liked this story, please leave a review at your retailer. Just a few words really helps!

IT'S NOT QUITE THE END!

Thank you so much for reading *The Billionaire's Secret*. The Billionaire's Secret was originally the fourth book in the Heartbeats Series title A Father's Love, but about the time I decided When Hearts Collide should be two stories, billionaires were huge. Max had already been written as rich and it was an easy switch to turn him into a billionaire and rebrand the cover.

The main story remains the same though and is one of my father's favorite books. I hope you enjoyed it as well. If you did, would you do me a favor? If you did, please leave a review at your retailer. It really helps. It doesn't have to be long - just a few words to help other readers know what they're getting.

I'd love to hear from you, not only about this story, but about the characters or stories you'd like read in the future. I'm always looking for new ideas and if I use one of your characters or stories, I'll send you a free ebook and paperback of the book with a special dedication. Write to me at loranahoopes@gmail.com. And if you'd like to see what's coming next, be sure to stop by authorloranahoopes.com

I also have a weekly newsletter that contains many wonderful things like pictures of my adorable children, chances to win awesome prizes, new releases and sales I might be holding, great books from other authors, and anything else that strikes my fancy and that I think you would enjoy. I'll even send you the first chapter of my newest (maybe not even released yet) book if you'd like to sign up.

Even better, I solemnly swear to only send out one newsletter a week (usually on Tuesday unless life gets in the way which with three kids it usually does). I will not spam you, sell your email address to solicitors or anyone else, or any of those other terrible things.

And if you're interested in meeting the rest of the billionaires in the series, be sure to check out A Brush with a Billionaire. Turn the page for a sneak peek.

NOT READY TO SAY GOODBYE YET?

Max and Alyssa will return in a later book, so you can check up on them, but until then, I hope you'll enjoy the next book in the series, Brush with a Billionaire. This book was originally a novella titled Love Breaks Through in the Kindle World, but when the Kindle World shut, we were given back the stories and I felt like Sam and Brent needed more.

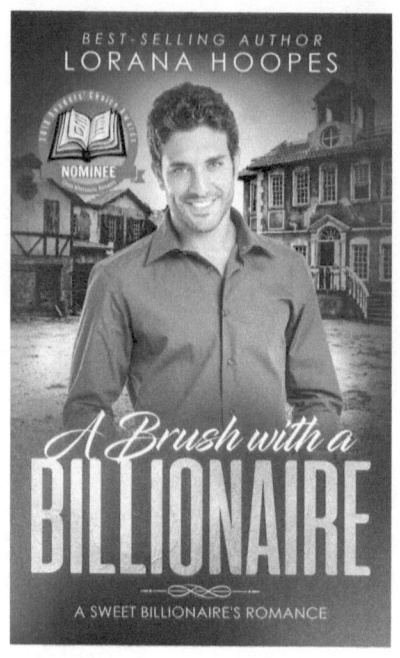

Brush with a Billionaire

He's an actor who wanted some time away...

Unfortunately, his car breaks down in a small town and he's forced to room with a stranger until it gets fixed

Alyssa Miller has been tasked with making sure Peyton is okay...

But dealing with Maxwell Banks is harder than she thought it would be and her issues with trust aren't helping.

A misunderstanding ....

May ruin everything Max has been working so hard for.

Read on for a taste of *The Billionaire's Secret*....

A BRUSH WITH A BILLIONAIRE PREVIEW

*D*ING!

As Brent glanced at the display, a stream of curses tumbled out of his mouth. This was the last thing he needed. The check engine light gleamed, its orange glow mocking him for not taking the car into the shop last month for its regular inspection. Usually, he was a stickler for those things, but he had just finished filming a movie and his most recent breakup, Tricia, had been blowing up his phone since the breakup. It was only natural that a small thing like car maintenance had slipped his mind.

And the timing was impeccable, of course. The last major city was approximately ten miles back, and nothing but sagebrush passed by his window now. Dusty, dirty, yellow and brown sagebrush. Why had he thought going to a cabin in the middle of nowhere would help him relax? Oh, right, it had been Julia's idea.

Julia had been his agent for years, so he knew better than to argue with her when she told him he needed to get away and take some time to regroup. It hadn't really been his fault he lost it with the most recent director. The script had been terrible, and Brent was tired of roles that held no substance. But, he should have rented a cabin in the mountains or the penthouse of some nice hotel on the beach. With his money, he could have afforded either and been closer to humanity. But no, Julia had insisted a cabin out in the middle of nowhere would be preferable.

"Come on, baby," he urged the Porsche, hoping they had a good enough relationship she would get him to the next town. The size didn't even matter as long as it had a working phone. His cell phone had lost reception after the last big town. A mechanic wouldn't hurt either.

"Stella, if you get me to the next town, I promise I'll take you to the best shop when we return." Brent had named her Stella after the girl he had been dating at the time - a high maintenance ex-girlfriend. The girl, a penthouse owning, designer wearing, Tiffany's lover hadn't lasted, but the car had, until now.

His hands glided over the grey leather covered steering wheel, sending positive energy and good thoughts to Stella. Perhaps his touch would spur her to limp another two miles to... what was the name on the last sign? Soda Spurs? An odd name for a town, but in Podunk Texas, he expected no less.

But, it was not to be. With a final stutter and a plume of blue smoke, Stella died on the side of Farm Market Road 1276. He glared at the asinine GPS that had recommended this shortcut in the first place and sighed. He should have stayed on the major highway. The city traffic was terrible, but at least a city would have guaranteed a tow truck and a mechanic in case of the unexpected. Now, he was stranded in the middle of nowhere with a hot, two-mile walk ahead of him.

As he popped the hood—hoping she had simply overheated and would work when she cooled down—more smoke billowed out from underneath. Brent was no mechanic, but smoke was never a good thing and probably meant a major fix. He checked the phone one more time in hopes the gods would show him pity, but it had no bars. *Useless!* It landed on the passenger seat as he swung open the car door.

The oppressive heat sent beads of sweat trickling down his back. Brent hated being sweaty unless he was at the gym. Even then, he always kept a towel close by. Salty stings in his eye while lifting heavy weights was not only annoying but dangerous.

He wiped a hand across his face before waving the smoke away and peering under the hood. A series of black and silver tubish things stared back at him, looking like a puzzle in a foreign language. He was not a car guy. Brent liked fancy cars – driving them, owning them, showing off in them, but he didn't care how they worked —that was why he paid other people. It was one of the many benefits of having money.

With a raised hand to shield his eyes, he scanned the road. Nothing but brown—unmoving, silent brown. A dirt plume at least would have meant a car was coming, but no dirt stirred along the road. He slammed the hood down.

With a heavy sigh, Brent snatched his worthless iPhone from the passenger seat, and jammed it back in his pocket. What good was having the latest technology if there were still parts of the state that had terrible service? Perhaps he needed to see about buying a few cell towers. There was a chance there would be cell reception in Soda Spurs though he doubted it.

He grabbed his laptop bag and then glanced into the backseat of the car to see if he needed to grab anything else, but there was nothing worth stealing there except his travel bag and it only held his clothes and toiletries.

A final thought urged him to grab the lukewarm bottle of water from the cup holder. His mouth turned down in disgust at the thought of swigging the warm liquid, but it was all he had.

After locking Stella, he flashed her one more longing

glance, slung his bag over his shoulder, and began the trek. The dust from the road soon covered his expensive black loafers, turning them an ashy color. He would have to purchase new ones when he returned to civilization.

Sweat pasted his short dark hair to his head, and beads ran in little rivulets down his back and sides. Stains developed under his arms, and the heat coupled with the weight of the bag rolled his shoulders forward. He would be sore tomorrow, but he pushed on.

Relief flooded him as the first signs of life appeared. Small run-down houses dotted the side of the road. The faded paint on them crackled and curled, and the boarded windows kept their secrets locked inside. His gold Rolex told him he had been walking for eighteen minutes though it felt much longer.

Another few minutes yielded a green sign welcoming him to Soda Spurs, TX. Population 5003. *5003?* He sighed, certain that many people lived in a city block alone in Houston, but the houses looked a little newer, not expensive, but more cared for, which ignited a small sliver of hope. Newer paint and open windows allowed the light breeze to flow in and rustle the curtains.

He approached a blue house with white trim where a lone figure rocked in a chair on the porch. The gray of her hair suggested an elderly age, but her hands nimbly moved the needles she worked as the chair tilted forward and back. It emitted an odd creaking sound in the silence of the street.

"Excuse me, ma'am." Brent poured out the charm his mother had taught him to use at a young age. He didn't have to use it as much now as people flocked to him because of his money, but he could still whip it out when necessary. "Can you tell me where I might find a phone or mechanic?"

She frowned at him, wrinkles crisscrossing her face, though the beauty underneath was still visible. In her youth, she must have broken hearts left and right. Her hands slowed as her eyes narrowed. Perhaps his charm had lost its touch, or else maybe his ragged appearance was causing her concern.

"I don't mean to scare you, ma'am. My car broke down about two miles back, and I had to walk. Is there anyone in this town who can help me? A mechanic or a tow place or something."

The stare continued another long minute before his answer seemed to satisfy her, and she leaned back in her rocker, needles clicking again. "Sam's auto shop is up the way. Turn left at the gnarled tree." Her leathery hand pointed to the right. "Norma's is on the way. She'll give you a bite to eat if you stop in. Tell her Fanny sent you."

Her head dropped back to whatever she was making in her lap, and the rocker began its rhythmic motion again. Brent raised his hand in a thank you, wishing he had a cowboy hat to tip her direction. He hadn't worn one in ages, not since leaving the small town he grew up in, but an image of his mother flustered and blushing as a man tipped his hat at her flashed into his mind. The cowboy hat held a mysterious power over some Texas women, and it would have come in handy now.

Brent continued his trek, sighing in relief when a white building on the left caught his eye. It was more like a house than a business as only the small sign spelling Norma's in faded red letters above the door informed him this was the restaurant. Three cars filled spaces around the house. A glance around revealed no gnarled tree so he turned into Norma's, hoping for better directions.

The cooler air smacked him as the door opened, sending a shiver racing along his spine. Two red booths and matching tables with red chairs filled most of the real estate in the room, which appeared to have once served as a dining room and living room.

The appearance outside had been deceptive as the inside was larger than he expected. Four stools, also upholstered in red fabric, sat in front of a large wooden bar. Rows of clear glasses lined several shelves behind the bar, and a drink dispenser that advertised Mr. Pibb and Mellow Yellow took up part of one wall. A cash register, the only newer contraption in the place, sat on the edge of the counter. At the far end of the room, a jukebox belted out an old country tune. Brent felt like he had traveled back in time.

All eyes in the place turned to him as the floor creaked beneath his feet, announcing his arrival. The room was not crowded. A man sat at the bar and a younger couple filled one booth. His eyes scanned the place, searching for the owner.

An older woman with short brown hair stepped out of the doorway he assumed led to the kitchen. A white towel was slung over her shoulder, and an apron, stained with many colors, hung on her waist.

"Can I help you?" she asked, wiping her hands on the apron.

"Yes ma'am. My car broke down a few miles outside town. I'm hoping you have a phone I can use as I can't get reception either." He pasted his best smile across his face—the one that got him any woman he wanted back home.

"Ain't got no phone, no use for one. Everyone here knows to come by if they need me." The woman shook her head once before turning back toward the kitchen.

"Wait." He stepped forward, his hand held out to her, though not too high. No sense in broadcasting his sweat stains. "I met Fanny, and she told me to find Norma. She also mentioned maybe Sam's shop could help get my car fixed."

Three pairs of eyes shifted from Brent back to the

woman as if watching a slow-motion tennis match on TV.

A small grin tugged at Norma's lips as she turned back. "Well, if Fanny sent you, you must be all right. Why don't you sit, and I'll get you something to eat?"

He had eaten in the last town. At a nice restaurant. With servers who wore black pants and white shirts and handed him a proper menu. The single sheet of paper kind attached to a hard background and filled with elegant writing. He doubted Norma's even had a menu or if it did, it would be one of those laminated atrocities that would make a sticky, suction sound as you pried it open.

The steak and salad at the restaurant had filled him up, but his stomach rumbled at the idea of food. Perhaps a dessert and a cold drink would hit the spot. Snagging an empty barstool, he collapsed in it and dropped his bag on the floor. "Do you have pie and iced tea, unsweetened?"

A tittering of laughter circled the room. "Do we have pie?" Norma asked placing her hands on her meaty hips. "Honey, we have apple pie, cherry pie, blueberry pie, pumpkin pie, and mincemeat pie." She ticked the names off on her fingers. "Norma is known for her pie. Though considering Soda Spurs was founded on an apple orchard, people say my apple pie is the best."

"You tell him, Norma," the man in the far corner shouted, lifting his fork in the air in salute.

"I'll have a slice of apple then." Brent had never liked fruit pies, but there was no way he would pick something else and risk offending the woman.

She disappeared into the kitchen and returned with a large slice of apple pie on a white china plate. Tiny wisps of steam rose from the combination of cold whip cream against the warm crust, and the aroma of apples and cinnamon reached his nose before she even set the plate in front of him. Based on the smell, he feared the taste would be overpowering. A small silver fork appeared next to the plate, and then Norma stepped back, crossed her arms, and waited.

A furtive glance around revealed everyone in the room watching him. Nothing like tasting something with an audience hanging on your every move. He hoped it either would be fantastic or that he'd be able to maintain a poker face if it didn't, for he believed they would throw him out if he showed any dislike for the pie. It was almost as if a stranger's acceptance among this group hung on his or her reaction to the pie.

The fork slid through the dessert, and he raised it to his mouth. As the small portion hit his tongue, a burst of flavors exploded in his mouth. It was the best apple pie he'd ever had, and his eyes widened in surprise. Cheers and clapping ensued as his lips turned up and he nodded before taking another bite. His reaction seemed to have appeased Norma as she then filled a cup with cold iced tea for him. Brent took a few long gulps before placing the cup back down. His throat felt as arid as the Sahara, but the cool liquid did its job.

"So, Fanny mentioned Sam's. Is it much farther?" he asked between bites. He would regret finishing this pie the next time he hit the gym, but for now he didn't care.

"Nah, it's jest a little ways up past the gnarled tree," the man to his right said. His denim overalls stretched across his large frame and a plain white t-shirt with visible sweat stains poked out. Day old stubble covered his face, and his hair was brown but thinning on top.

"Does it have a street name?"

"I reckon, but no one round here uses it, so I can't rightly say I remember what it is." He picked up a toothpick and chewed on it.

"Don't mind Paul here." Norma shot a look at the stout man. "This is the outskirts of Soda Spurs. The main town has street names. Sam's is about a block up. If you get to Willow Street, you've gone too far."

"Thanks." He downed another gulp of tea and pushed the cleaned plate toward her. "How much do I owe you?"

Her hand flicked in dismissal. "First one's on the house. I can't have you passing out from hunger and dehydration. Marnie and Ernest would have my hide."

Another laugh erupted, and Brent forced a smile though he didn't understand what she meant. However, he knew from experience that small towns held many inside jokes.

"Well, thank you again." His legs buckled as he stood and he had to grip the counter to remain standing. They were still a little rubbery from the long walk. The reprieve had been nice. When all the feeling came back into them, he raised his hand in a wave, shouldered his bag again, and headed out the door.

Scorching heat beat down on him again as he stepped out of the air-conditioned diner, and his shoulder protested the weight of his bag. The reprieve had been nice. He should have asked for a bottle of water, but it had sounded like this Sam's place wasn't much farther. Perhaps, he would have water.

As the gnarled tree came into view, Brent could see why they used it as a marker. It was grey and twisted as if cursed with some ancient magic, and nothing was around it. There was no street sign marker, so if it had a name, it was keeping it secret.

Down this street were a few houses, painted in tans and beiges. They almost blended into the background. Up ahead, the small converted shop appeared among the neighborhood houses. He couldn't imagine the shop could hold more than one car at a time, but it probably didn't need to. He hadn't heard or seen a car driving in this town.

S A M' S was stenciled across the front door. As he pushed open the door, a bell jingled above his head announcing his arrival.

No one manned the cluttered counter, so he stepped into the large opening that led to the shop to the left. An old green Ford truck filled the space, and at the front of the truck, he spied two denim legs.

"Hello?" he asked. "I'm looking for Sam."

The legs rolled out from under the car until the full person was exposed. His heart stalled in his chest. Sam was not the greasy male mechanic he expected, but a petite brunette, though she was sporting a grease smear across her cheek. Her dark blue jumpsuit was large and hung on her body, hiding the curves he imagined lay underneath.

"I'm Sam. What can I do for you?" She wiped her hand on a red towel she pulled from her pocket as she met his gaze. Her blue eyes reminded him of the sky when no clouds filled it.

"But … you're a woman." The shocked words spilled out of his mouth before he could stop them.

Her eyebrow inched up her forehead as her arms crossed and leaned back. "Yeah, I'm a woman. You got a problem with that?"

He did, on so many levels. A woman could not

possibly fix his Porsche, but he'd already ruffled her feathers. If nothing else, perhaps she would order whatever part he needed, and recommend a real mechanic.

Brent swallowed his pride and issued a lackluster apology. "No, I'm sorry. It's ... I was expecting a man." Her sky-blue eyes continued to glare at him, waiting for a better explanation. "My car broke down outside of town, and I was hoping you could fix it or order a part or something."

Her gaze traveled the length of his body as if sizing him up. "What kind of car?"

"Porsche 911."

A snort escaped her mouth. "Figures."

Irritation flared within him. "I beg your pardon?"

"Figures you would drive such an uppity car. I could tell by the way you're dressed."

He bit his tongue to keep the reply he wanted to spew back at her in check. A few hasty generalizations on her outfit and the fact that she lived in this small town flooded his mind, but he needed her help. With great effort, he swallowed the vinegar and opted to pour out honey instead.

"You got me. I live in Houston, but I was hoping to get away from the noise and relax. Can you help me?" He flashed his best puppy dog eyes at her, hoping they would work as well on her as they had on other women.

"Fine. I'll look at your snobby car. Follow me."

With a quick spin, she led the way through a back door where a faded blue Chevy truck waited.

Continue reading Brush With a Billionaire....

Or get the boxed set with 3 books and save!

A FREE STORY FOR YOU

𝓔njoyed this story? Not ready to quit reading yet? If you sign up for my newsletter, you will receive The Billionaire's Impromptu Bet right away as my thank you gift for choosing to hang out with me.

The Billionaire's Impromptu Bet

A SWAT officer. A bored billionaire heiress. A bet that could change everything....

Read on for a taste of The Billionaire's Impromptu Bet....

*B*rie Carter fell back spread eagle on her queen-sized canopy bed sending her blond hair fanning out behind her. With a large sigh, she uttered, "I'm bored."

"How can you be bored? You have like millions of dollars." Her friend, Ariel, plopped down in a seated position on the bed beside her and flicked her raven hair off her shoulder. "You want to go shopping? I hear Tiffany's is having a special right now."

Brie rolled her eyes. Shopping? Where was the excitement in that? With her three platinum cards, she could go shopping whenever she wanted. "No, I'm bored with shopping too. I have everything. I want to do something exciting. Something we don't normally do."

Brie enjoyed being rich. She loved the unlimited

credit cards at her disposal, the constant apparel of new clothes, and of course the penthouse apartment her father paid for, but lately, she longed for something more fulfilling.

Ariel's hazel eyes widened. "I know. There's a new bar down on Franklin Street. Why don't we go play a little game?"

Brie sat up, intrigued at the secrecy and the twinkle in Ariel's eyes. "What kind of game?"

"A betting game. You let me pick out any man in the place. Then you try to get him to propose to you."

Brie wrinkled her nose. "But I don't want to get married." She loved her freedom and didn't want to share her penthouse with anyone, especially some man.

"You don't marry him, silly. You just get him to propose."

Brie bit her lip as she thought. It had been awhile since her last relationship and having a man dote on her for a month might be interesting, but…. "I don't know. It doesn't seem very nice."

"How about I sweeten the pot? If you win, I'll set you up on a date with my brother."

Brie cocked her head. Was she serious? The only thing Brie couldn't seem to buy in the world was the affection of Ariel's very handsome, very wealthy, brother. He was a movie star, just the kind of person Brie could consider marrying in the future. She'd had a crush on him as long as she and Ariel had been friends, but he'd always seen her as just that, his little sister's friend. "I thought you didn't want me dating your brother."

"I don't." Ariel shrugged. "But he's between girlfriends right now, and I know you've wanted it for ages. If you win this bet, I'll set you up. I can't guarantee any more than one date though. The rest will be up to you."

Brie wasn't worried about that. Charm she possessed in abundance. She simply needed some alone time with him, and she was certain she'd be able to convince him they were meant to be together. "All right. You've got a deal."

Ariel smiled. "Perfect. Let's get you changed then and see who the lucky man will be."

A tiny tug pulled on Brie's heart that this still wasn't right, but she dismissed it. This was simply a means to an end, and he'd never have to know.

❧

*J*esse Calhoun relaxed as the rhythmic thudding of the speed bag reached his ears. Though he loved his job, it was stressful being the SWAT sniper. He hated having to take human lives and today had been especially rough. The team had been called out to a drug bust, and Jesse was forced to return fire at three hostiles. He didn't care that they fired at his team and himself first. Taking a life was always hard, and every one of them haunted his dreams.

"You gonna bust that one too?" His co-worker Brendan appeared by his side. Brendan was the opposite of Jesse in nearly every way. Where Jesse's hair was a dark copper, Brendan's was nearly black. Jesse sported paler skin and a dusting of freckles across his nose, but Brendan's skin was naturally dark and freckle free.

Jesse flashed a crooked grin, but kept his eyes on the small, swinging black bag. The speed bag was his way to release, but a few times he had started hitting while still too keyed up and he had ruptured the bag. Okay, five times, but who was counting really? Besides, it was a better way to calm his nerves than other things he could choose. Drinking, fights, gambling, women.

"Nah, I think this one will last a little longer." His shoulders began to burn, and he gave the bag another few punches for good measure before dropping his arms and letting it swing to a stop. "See? It lives to be hit at least another day." Every once in a while, Jesse missed training the way he used to. Before he joined the force, he had been an amateur boxer, on his way to being a pro, but a shoulder injury had delayed his training and forced him to consider something else. It had eventually healed, but by then he had lost his edge.

"Hey, why don't you come drink with us?" Brendan

clapped a hand on Jesse's shoulder as they headed into the locker room.

"You know I don't drink." Jesse often felt like the outsider of the team. While half of the six-man team was married, the other half found solace in empty bottles and meaningless relationships. Jesse understood that - their job was such that they never knew if they would come home night after night - but he still couldn't partake.

Brendan opened his locker and pulled out a clean shirt. He peeled off his current one and added deodorant before tugging on the new one. "You don't have to drink. Look, I won't drink either. Just come and hang out with us. You have no one waiting for you at home."

That wasn't entirely true. Jesse had Bugsy, his Boston Terrier, but he understood Brendan's point. Most days, Jesse went home, fed Bugsy, made dinner, and fell asleep watching TV on the couch. It wasn't much of a life. "All right, I'll go, but I'm not drinking."

Brendan's lips pulled back to reveal his perfectly white teeth. He bragged about them, but Jesse knew they were veneers. "That's the spirit. Hurry up and change. We don't want to leave the rest of the team waiting."

"Is everyone coming?" Jesse pulled out his shower necessities. Brendan might feel comfortable going out with just a new application of deodorant, but Jesse needed to wash more than just dirt and sweat off. He needed to wash the sound of the bullets and the sight of lifeless bodies from his mind.

"Yeah, Pat's wife is pregnant again and demanding some crazy food concoctions. Pat agreed to pick them up if she let him have an hour. Cam and Jared's wives are having a girls' night, so the whole gang can be together. It will be nice to hang out when we aren't worried about being shot at."

"Fine. Give me ten minutes. Unlike you, I like to clean up before I go out."

Brendan smirked. "I've never had any complaints. Besides, do you know how long it takes me to get my hair like this?"

Jesse shook his head as he walked into the shower, but he knew it was true. Brendan had rugged good looks and muscles to match. He rarely had a hard time finding a woman. Jesse on the other hand hadn't dated anyone in the last few months. It wasn't that he hadn't been looking, but he was quieter than his teammates. And he wasn't looking for right now. He was looking for forever. He just hadn't found it yet.

Click here to continue reading The Billionaire's Impromptu Bet.

THE STORY DOESN'T END!

You've met a few people and fallen in love....

I bet you're wondering how you can meet everyone else.

Star Lake Series:

Sealed with a Kiss: Meet the quirky cast of Star Lake and find out if Max and Layla will ever find love.

When Love Returns: Return to Star Lake to hear Presley's story and find out if she gets the second chance with her first love.

Once Upon a Star: Continue the journey when aspiring actress Audrey returns home with a baby. Will Blake finally get the nerve to share his feelings with her?

Love Conquers All: Meet Lanie Perkins Hall who never imagined being divorced at thirty or falling for an old friend, but will his secrets keep them apart?

The Star Lake Collection: Get the latter three stories in one place. Series will include book 1 when it releases around November 2020.

The Heartbeats Series:

Where It All Began: Sandra Baker finds forgiveness and healing even after making a horrible choice.

The Power of Prayer: Will Callie Green find true love or be defined by her mistake?

When Hearts Collide: When Amanda Adams goes to college, she finds a world she was not ready for. But will she also find true love?

A Past Forgiven: Jess Peterson has lived a life of abuse and lost her self worth, but when she finds herself pregnant, will she find new hope?

The Heartbeats Collection: Grab all four Heartbeats novels in one collection

Sweet Billionaires Series:

The Billionaire's Impromptu Bet: Can a spoiled rich girl change when a bet turns to love?

The Billionaire's Secret: Can a playboy settle down when he finds out he has a daughter who needs him?

A Brush with a Billionaire: What happens when a stuck up actor lands in a small town and needs help from a female mechanic?

The Billionaire's Christmas Miracle: A twist on a Cinderella story when a billionaire meets a woman who doesn't belong at the ball.

The Billionaire's Cowboy Groom: Will one night six years ago keep Carrie from finding true love?

The Cowboy Billionaire: Coming Soon!

The Billionaire's Bliss: This collection contains The Billionaire's Secret, The Billionaire's Christmas Miracle, and The Billionaire's Cowboy Groom

The Lawkeeper Series:

Lawfully Matched: When the man she agreed to marry turns out to have a dark past, will Kate have to return home or will she find love with her rescuer in this historical fiction?

Lawfully Justified: Can a bounty hunter and a widow find love together in this historical fiction?

The Scarlet Wedding: William and Emma are planning their wedding, but an outbreak and a return from his past force them to change their plans. Is a happily ever after still in their future in this historical fiction?

Lawfully Redeemed: What happens when a K9 cop falls for the brother of her suspect? Contemporary romance.

The Lawkeeper Collection: Get all four books in one collection

The Are You Listening Series:

The Still Small Voice: Will Jordan listen to God's prompting in this speculative fiction?

A Spark in the Darkness Will Jordan be able to help Raven before the rapture occurs?

Blushing Brides Series:

The Cowboy's Reality Bride: He's agreed to be the bachelor on a reality dating show, but what happens when he falls for a woman who's not one of the contestants?

The Reality Bride's Baby: Laney wants nothing more than a baby, but when she starts feeling dizzy is it pregnancy or something more serious?

The Producer's Unlikely Bride: What happens when a producer and an author agree to a fake relationship?

Ava's Blessing in Disguise: Five years after marriage, Ava faces a mysterious illness that threatens to ruin her career. Will she find out what it is?

The Soldier's Steadfast Bride: coming soon

The Men of Fire Beach

Fire Games: Cassidy returns home from Who Wants to Marry a Cowboy to find obsessive letters from a fan. The cop assigned to help her wants to get back to his case, but what she sees at a fire may just be the key he's looking for.

Lost Memories and New Beginnings: A doctor, a patient with no memory, the men out to get her. Can he keep her safe when he doesn't know who he's looking for?

When Questions Abound: A Companion story to Lost Memories. Told from Detective Graves' point of view.

Never Forget the Past: Fireman Bubba must confront his past in order to clear his name and save lives.

Love on the Run: Graham is forced into lockdown with one of his employees. Will he be able to save her from her ex and will she steal his heart?

Secrets and Suspense: Cara Hunter is hiding something about her military past. When she's suspected of murder, will she be able to convince Cole she's the victim?

The Men of Fire Beach Collection: Books 1-3

Texas Tornadoes

Defending My Heart: Forced to confront his past, Emmitt finds news that will change his life.

Run With My Heart: Sentenced to community service, Tucker finds himself falling for the manager.

Love on the Line: Blaine has hired Kenzi to redo his cabin, but what happens when she finds his darkest secret?

Touchdown on Love: When Mason's injury throws him together with ex-girlfriend, will sparks fly again?

Second Chance Reception: Jefferson is hiding something. When he falls for the team cook, will he let her in?

Small Town Short Stories

Small Town Dreams

Small Town Second Chances

Small Town Rivals

Small Town Life

Life in a Small Town: All four stories in one collection

Stand Alones:

Love Renewed: This books is part of the multi author second chance series. When fate reunites high school sweethearts separated by life's choices, can they find a second chance at love at a snowy lodge amid a little mystery?

Her children's early reader chapter book series:

The Wishing Stone #1: Dangerous Dinosaur

The Wishing Stone #2: Dragon Dilemma

The Wishing Stone #3: Mesmerizing Mermaids

The Wishing Stone #4: Pyramid Puzzle

The Wishing Stone: Mary's Miracle

The Wishing Stone Collection
To see a list of all her books

authorloranahoopes.com
loranahoopes@gmail.com

ABOUT THE AUTHOR

Lorana Hoopes is an inspirational author originally from Texas but now living in the PNW with her husband and three children. When not writing, she can be seen kickboxing at the gym, singing, or acting on stage. One day, she hopes to retire from teaching and write full time.

THE STORY DOESN'T END!

You've met a few people and fallen in love….

I bet you're wondering how you can meet everyone else.

Star Lake Series:

Sealed with a Kiss: Meet the quirky cast of Star Lake and find out if Max and Layla will ever find love.

When Love Returns: Return to Star Lake to hear Presley's story and find out if she gets the second chance with her first love.

Once Upon a Star: Continue the journey when aspiring actress Audrey returns home with a baby. Will Blake finally get the nerve to share his feelings with her?

Love Conquers All: Meet Lanie Perkins Hall who never imagined being divorced at thirty or falling for an old friend, but will his secrets keep them apart?

The Star Lake Collection: Get the latter three stories in one place. Series will include book 1 when it releases around November 2020.

The Heartbeats Series:

Where It All Began: Sandra Baker finds forgiveness and healing even after making a horrible choice.

The Power of Prayer: Will Callie Green find true love or be defined by her mistake?

When Hearts Collide: When Amanda Adams goes to college, she finds a world she was not ready for. But will she also find true love?

A Past Forgiven: Jess Peterson has lived a life of abuse and lost her self worth, but when she finds herself pregnant, will she find new hope?

The Heartbeats Collection: Grab all four Heartbeats novels in one collection

Sweet Billionaires Series:

The Billionaire's Impromptu Bet: Can a spoiled rich girl change when a bet turns to love?

The Billionaire's Secret: Can a playboy settle down when he finds out he has a daughter who needs him?

A Brush with a Billionaire: What happens when a stuck up actor lands in a small town and needs help from a female mechanic?

The Billionaire's Christmas Miracle: A twist

on a Cinderella story when a billionaire meets a woman who doesn't belong at the ball.

The Billionaire's Cowboy Groom: Will one night six years ago keep Carrie from finding true love?

The Cowboy Billionaire: Coming Soon!

The Billionaire's Bliss: This collection contains The Billionaire's Secret, The Billionaire's Christmas Miracle, and The Billionaire's Cowboy Groom

The Lawkeeper Series:

Lawfully Matched: When the man she agreed to marry turns out to have a dark past, will Kate have to return home or will she find love with her rescuer in this historical fiction?

Lawfully Justified: Can a bounty hunter and a widow find love together in this historical fiction?

The Scarlet Wedding: William and Emma are planning their wedding, but an outbreak and a return from his past force them to change their plans. Is a happily ever after still in their future in this historical fiction?

Lawfully Redeemed: What happens when a K9 cop falls for the brother of her suspect? Contemporary romance.

The Lawkeeper Collection: Get all four books in one collection

The Are You Listening Series:

The Still Small Voice: Will Jordan listen to God's prompting in this speculative fiction?

A Spark in the Darkness Will Jordan be able to help Raven before the rapture occurs?

Blushing Brides Series:

The Cowboy's Reality Bride: He's agreed to be the bachelor on a reality dating show, but what happens when he falls for a woman who's not one of the contestants?

The Reality Bride's Baby: Laney wants nothing more than a baby, but when she starts feeling dizzy is it pregnancy or something more serious?

The Producer's Unlikely Bride: What happens when a producer and an author agree to a fake relationship?

Ava's Blessing in Disguise: Five years after marriage, Ava faces a mysterious illness that threatens to ruin her career. Will she find out what it is?

The Soldier's Steadfast Bride: coming soon

The Men of Fire Beach

Fire Games: Cassidy returns home from Who Wants to Marry a Cowboy to find obsessive letters from a fan. The cop assigned to help her wants to get back to his case, but what she sees at a fire may just be the key he's looking for.

Lost Memories and New Beginnings: A doctor, a patient with no memory, the men out to get her. Can he keep her safe when he doesn't know who he's looking for?

When Questions Abound: A Companion story to Lost Memories. Told from Detective Graves' point of view.

Never Forget the Past: Fireman Bubba must confront his past in order to clear his name and save lives.

Love on the Run: Graham is forced into lockdown with one of his employees. Will he be able to save her from her ex and will she steal his heart?

Secrets and Suspense: Cara Hunter is hiding something about her military past. When she's suspected of murder, will she be able to convince Cole she's the victim?

The Men of Fire Beach Collection: Books 1-3

Texas Tornadoes

Defending My Heart: Forced to confront his past, Emmitt finds news that will change his life.

Run With My Heart: Sentenced to community service, Tucker finds himself falling for the manager.

Love on the Line: Blaine has hired Kenzi to redo his cabin, but what happens when she finds his darkest secret?

Touchdown on Love: When Mason's injury throws him together with ex-girlfriend, will sparks fly again?

Second Chance Reception: Jefferson is hiding something. When he falls for the team cook, will he let her in?

Small Town Short Stories

Small Town Dreams

Small Town Second Chances

Small Town Rivals

Small Town Life

Life in a Small Town: All four stories in one collection

Stand Alones:

Love Renewed: This books is part of the multi author second chance series. When fate reunites high school sweethearts separated by life's choices, can they find a second chance at love at a snowy lodge amid a little mystery?

Her children's early reader chapter book series:

The Wishing Stone #1: Dangerous Dinosaur

The Wishing Stone #2: Dragon Dilemma

The Wishing Stone #3: Mesmerizing Mermaids

The Wishing Stone #4: Pyramid Puzzle

The Wishing Stone Inspirations 1: Mary's Miracle

To see a list of all her books

authorloranahoopes.com

loranahoopes@gmail.com

ABOUT THE AUTHOR

Lorana Hoopes is an inspirational author originally from Texas but now living in the PNW with her husband and three children. When not writing, she can be seen kickboxing at the gym, singing, or acting on stage. One day, she hopes to retire from teaching and write full time.